WHISPERS FROM THE PAST

Written by Catherine LaCroix

Artwork by Marlena Mozgawa

STORIES IN THIS COMPILATION:

Roar

Remember

React

Raucous

THE SEQUEL TO

THE WHISPERS OF RINGS

ISBN: 978-1974245383

LaCroix Publishing

www.whispersfromcat.wordpress.com

For Natsuki and Pete

The Kingdom of Rhoryn

THE KINGDOM OF ORDEHL

MYRIN

LAKE OF THE GODDESS

MAURA

VERITAS

LORELYN

THE CAPITAL

THE ISTEN MOUNTAINS

BONAS RIVER

VALFORD

THE VERDANT THICKET

ANASTAS

CITY OF ENDS

ROAR

BOOK ONE
OF
WHISPERS FROM THE PAST

I

It was an inconsequential evening that changed the entire course of my life. I couldn't say the day or the time, but I remember it was snowing.

I was restless, inconsolable, and suffered from the curiosities of childhood. I'm sure my mother knew of my late night escapes but never said a word. The moon washed over the snow in a gleam that would draw envy from the sun as I padded my way over the white landscape. It was late; far later than any eight-year-old should have wandered from their room. But I couldn't sleep and nothing in my home seemed to distract my fits of insomnia.

And so I wandered. The powdered streets of Lorelyn were abandoned at such a late hour. The chill air sometimes calmed the thoughts that rushed through my head—thoughts that should have never weighed me down to begin with.

That's when I saw you.

Dark hair succumbed to the wills of the breeze, bright eyes sparkled in time with the stars. You perched beneath an old oak tree, staring intently at the Isten Mountains. With the wisdom and courage of a child, I approached, taking a seat next to you.

"What are you looking at?" I asked, oblivious to the social anxieties I would learn later.

"I'm…wondering what's past the Istens," you replied with the graces of one a few years older than I.

With the all-encompassing knowledge of someone who hasn't been told that there are things that simply don't exist, I told you with outright confidence: "There's dragons out there."

You laughed and my tenacity shattered.

I poked at a few pebbles in the snow, avoiding your beautiful gaze and hiding my embarrassment. I wasn't yet to be bested. "Well, you don't know. What if there are?"

"What if there are?" you replied, nodding and hiding your giggles. "What's your name?"

"Cyprus Reyner," I announced proudly, as my parents had taught me. *Never fear who you are*, they'd said. "And yours?"

"Victoria d'Audrieu," you declared easily, your name rolling off of your tongue like a melody. "Well met."

"Well…met," I responded slowly, unassociated with the phrase. "What's out there for you?"

"Hmm," you contemplated my question with more credence than it was worth. "A prince to save me, a world to see, cities far larger than this…"

"I'll take the dragons," I responded with distaste, familiar with the fairy tales mothers told their daughters.

"Would you fight them, Cyprus?" you asked without missing a beat.

"Of course!" I responded with the fervor of a brave knight.

"Why?"

And, my love, that's where you had me. *Why?* For fame? For glory?

"I…Well, someone would have to lead you to your prince, right?"

You laughed and it was the most beautiful sound I'd ever heard in my short existence.

I shivered and you positioned yourself so your cloak covered us both. Your skin warmed me, your laugh warmed me—everything about you warmed my entire being.

"My parents…they've always told me to stay away from Whispers," you remarked while you pulled me closer to you.

I knew what I was; everyone knew what I was. But you so freely commented on something I'd never been ashamed of before. For a few span of seconds, I wondered if I should be. "Why?"

"I don't know," you said, pushing back a strand of hair that fell across my eyes. "You're quite sweet."

"Can we be friends, Victoria?" My hopes peaked as I leaned into you.

"I'd like that very much," you smiled—it made the snow jealous.

We watched the moon disappear over the Istens. Together.

II

After a few sleepless evenings of meeting Victoria beneath what I'd christened "our tree," I couldn't hide my exhaustion. One morning after my father made his way to work, my mother sat down with me at our small dining table and passed me a mug.

"It's hot. Make sure you sip it." She cradled her own cup between her hands.

"Hot chocolate?" No amount of sleep deprivation could hide my excitement.

We only had hot chocolate on special occasions—the price of cocoa in Lorelyn was outrageous.

"That it is, dearest." She smiled, deepening the lines in the corners of her eyes and mouth. Guinevere Reyner loved with all her heart and laughed without inhibition. "I know you've been out the past few nights."

I had the decency to look guilty. "I…um…"

"I know you have a hard time sleeping sometimes. Your mother is just worried. That's all."

"I made a friend," I admitted, sipping on my rare treat.

"You did?" Her blue eyes sparkled. I wasn't known for my social circle. "And who would that be?"

don't understand. Maybe they've only heard scary stories of them in books or fairy tales, or by word of mouth. But, maybe they never gave the thing they're afraid of an opportunity to prove how it is in reality. That it doesn't act out of malice. That maybe it doesn't roar at *them*, but for something greater."

I thought on her words, considering them one by one. People just had to give me a chance? I would impress them as much as possible.

"I'll be a dragon who doesn't roar!" It was the best solution I could muster. If dragons were perceived as kinder without roaring, then I could exist as a Whisper without causing unease.

"There you are." She smiled, finishing her drink. "You'll be the one to change their minds."

"Thanks, Mom! I'll be back later!" I polished off my hot chocolate before running outside into the snow, destination unknown.

My attentions were short and excitement lay in the outdoors. My mother understood, occasionally keeping an eye to the outside and trusted that I would always return safely. I always did.

The following afternoon, I paced the living room waiting for Victoria to arrive. I was excited and nervous, wondering what she would think of my home.

My mother watched me from the kitchen with patient amusement. When the knock finally came, she wiped her hands on her apron and moved to the door.

I positioned myself at her side, wringing my hands in an effort to keep myself occupied.

She opened the door and a light draft carried into our warm house, bringing with it a few flakes of snow.

Victoria stood beside a tall, slim woman that could only be her mother—identical eyes and hair—and curtsied kindly. "It's nice to meet you, Lady Reyner. I'm Victoria d'Audrieu, and this is my mother, Madeline d'Audrieu."

"Call me Gwen, please," my mother replied, offering a curtsy of her own.

"This must be Cyprus," Madeline remarked. Her tone was curious, her eyes were quizzical.

For the first time in my life, I realized I was being measured.

The cautions of Victoria's parents played through my mind again. *Stay away from Whispers.*

But…I was a dragon who didn't roar.

"It's a pleasure to meet you." I gave her a sweeping bow, taking Madeline's hand and kissing the top of it.

It was something I'd witnessed my father do when he took me into town. I associated it with being a gentleman.

To my surprise, Madeline laughed and tousled my hair.

My pride was hurt, I wondered if I'd executed it incorrectly.

"Would both of you like to come in? I've just finished making tea and snacks," my mother offered.

"Thank you for the offer. Unfortunately, I'm afraid I have to help my husband clean up his shop. I would love to accept in the future, though."

"Not a problem at all. The offer stands, then."

"Behave yourself, Victoria. I'll be back this evening to walk you home." Madeline kissed Victoria's forehead.

"I always do, Mother." Victoria's voice was sweet, but I caught her eyes rolling.

We ushered her in and waved Madeline off.

"Where'd you learn a bow like that?" Mother asked.

"I saw dad do it once. It didn't seem like it worked for me," I replied.

"You're a little heartbreaker, love. It worked." Her words mended my ego.

"So your father's a teacher?" Victoria asked me. We'd talked about it briefly the night before when I'd invited her to my home.

"He teaches history and language at the university. He said Mom would start us off and he'll help us when he gets home." I took a pastry and mug of tea, seating myself at the table.

"Is he a Whisper, too?" she asked casually.

I saw Mother glance between us, but I was too young to understand her concern. Victoria was too young to understand why it was a controversial question.

"No, my grandpa was. I don't really remember him, though." My grandfather on my mother's side had the blood of a Whisper and so did she, despite her appearance. My skin was caramel colored and hair bright white in contrast to her soft, pale hues.

"When Cyprus was very little, my father came down with a terrible illness. We did all we could but…he passed on even so." Mother would often tell me stories of her childhood that made me wish I would have known my grandfather better. I wasn't given the time.

"I'm sorry. I didn't mean to bring up negative—"

"No, you didn't. It's quite alright. He lives on through my memories." Mother smiled and nibbled on one of the baked goods as Victoria stared into her tea. Mother then tactfully changed the subject. "Are you two really prepared to learn a whole new language?"

"I've never been more excited," Victoria replied, her eyes sparkling.

I had to agree with her, the thought of a new means to speak with someone entranced me.

"Let's start!" I chimed in.

I took to Alavei as a bird takes to flight. It felt natural on my tongue and my parents were wonderful teachers. I loved the mechanics of it: the grammar, the nuances, the pronunciations that separated the language from the Reln I'd grown up with. When my father took over teaching from my mother, he was ecstatic to find two so young interested in learning. He helped perfect our accents and emphasis and was able to break down the hows and whys of the order of words.

Victoria struggled with some of the phrases and certain words didn't gracefully roll off her tongue as they would in Reln. This served to fuel my own personal education. I stayed up late into the night with my father, learning more, practicing more—just so that I could help Victoria as much as possible. He brought us spare parchment from the university to practice on. Mine was always filled in a few days' time.

Madeline walked Victoria to our home any day that Victoria's schedule wasn't filled with other lessons—music, etiquette, and sewing. Compared to our study of language, Victoria's daily life seemed so boring to me. I wondered how she could stand it. Oftentimes, Madeline would stay for tea and speak with my mother about small things and I took those opportunities to engage her as much as possible. Even if I wasn't incredibly interested in her answers, I'd ask her about her home, their cat, her husband's— Simon's—shop, anything to provoke her into talking to me. At first, her answers were strained and short, but over the years she warmed up to me and held full conversations. Eventually, Victoria showed up on my doorstep each morning without the watchful eye of her mother. Madeline would only join when she wanted to spend some time speaking with my mother. I didn't meet her father until Victoria's sixteenth nameday and even then he spared me a short word and a cautious glance.

After I mastered Alavei at the age of thirteen, my father suggested I learn a new, nearly forgotten language. It used long strokes that represented entire words as opposed to singular letters to make up an alphabet. It was much more difficult than Alavei or Reln, and I accepted the challenge with fervor. Each day Victoria visited, I would pause in my studies to continue teaching her Alavei.

One evening a few weeks before my own sixteenth birthday, my mother pulled me aside. We sat on the floor of my room, just the two of us. She handed me a mug of hot chocolate—it would forever be my guilty pleasure.

"Cyprus, you're nearly an adult now and there are...some things we should talk about," she began. "Like, what it means to be a Whisper."

"Alright," I nodded, wondering what she could possibly tell me that I didn't already know.

"I promised my father that I'd relay everything he told me before he passed when I thought you were ready. I know how much Victoria means to you and I don't want you to unintentionally hurt her."

I blushed and looked to the floor, was I that obvious? "I would never hurt her."

"I know, love, and that's one of your best qualities." She brushed the hair from my eyes and tipped my chin up so her gaze met mine. "We'll start with something a little easier. Whispers share a common creed. *Tere L'etai.* Love Freely."

"What...does that even mean?"

"It's meant to exist to help understand who you are and what you want as a person. From what I gleaned of my father, you aren't bound by the rules of gods on who you choose to love and how. You have the capability of... of loving more than one person at once, you see."

What she said seemed impossible. I could never care for anyone more than I cared for Victoria. "I'm not sure I could do that."

"It's not a requirement. It simply means you have the capacity to. Not that you must." Mother paused for a moment and I took a sip of the still scalding hot chocolate. "I have a feeling I can spare you the details on the basics of sex—"

"Mother, please." This conversation seemed focused around making me as embarrassed as possible. I had access to hundreds of books thanks to my father. Of course I knew.

"Cyprus, I wouldn't bring this up if it wasn't important. Your grandfather told me he wished someone was there to tell him these things. You need to know the sensations you're subject to."

"Like what?" I took another drink, trying not to meet her eyes. I understood that she was right. It was just difficult to talk to my own Mother about my body.

"There are certain things you'll react dramatically to that a normal person wouldn't. Like your sense of touch, smell, and sound. It can be *very* easy to lose yourself in any one of them."

"Lose myself...As in losing control of myself?" It was hard to believe that at any point I wouldn't be able to maintain self-control.

"Yes, that's exactly what I mean. Let's say you hear a melody you really enjoy. Your whole being becomes solely dedicated to listening to that song. Then, once it's over, you want nothing more than to hear it again. To the point that it may drive you mad if you don't. You *need* to hear this song. Imagine that feeling, but...replace a melody with the touch of another person."

I enjoyed Victoria's company immensely, but I couldn't imagine craving her as a necessity. The thought in itself scared me. I stared into my mug and wondered if I was born a monster. It was no wonder her parents wanted her to stay away from Whispers—

we were desperate for the companionship. And to what end? They were afraid of me.

"What's on your mind, sweet?" She interrupted my thoughts.

"I...I don't want to be feared. I don't want to hurt her...So, what can I do?"

"Don't ever be ashamed of who you are. I've told you that for years and I mean it. You don't want to hurt Victoria and you won't. Just because some people fear you doesn't mean that you're meant to be feared. A...dragon who doesn't roar, isn't that right?"

"I...Yes." She remembered what I'd said from so many years before. No matter the circumstances, I was still myself. Whatever instincts I harnessed, I refused to let them change me. "I won't be feared."

"Good," she sighed. We shared a few beats of silence before she said anything more. "Did I add enough cinnamon to your drink this time?"

"Cinnamon?" I laughed in spite of myself.

"That's the secret ingredient! I'm surprised you never noticed." She leaned in and kissed my cheek. "I love you. If you ever need to talk to me about any of this, please don't be afraid to?"

"Of course, Mom. I love you too." I smiled and drained my mug.

Tere L'etai...

III

On my sixteenth nameday, the day I was considered a full-fledged adult, both my family and Victoria surprised me. The spring had melted the last of the winter's snow and Lorelyn's flowers were blooming in sporadic patches along the roads. The aromas of breakfast dragged me from sleep and I slipped on my trousers before going into the kitchen.

"That smells delicious," I mumbled, rubbing the sleep from my eyes.

"Cyprus, I'm sorry. I should have told you…" My mother was trying not to laugh, and I didn't understand why.

Victoria cleared her throat. I jumped in surprise—I didn't expect her so early, if at all. I slowly realized I hadn't bothered to find a shirt.

She focused on her cup of tea, but I caught the quick dart of her eyes.

"I'm sorry, Victoria, I didn't think—" I could feel the heat of embarrassment rising to my face.

"No, I wanted to surprise you. It's my fault." She was trying to hide it—the mischievous little smile she saved for me when she was up to something.

"Go get dressed and then come eat with us." Mother laughed, shooing me away with a spoon.

Withholding the panic that overcame me, I marched back to my room to find a tunic. Victoria's glances and her smile brought more than the heat of embarrassment to my blood—a new sensation I wasn't familiar with. I breathed and suppressed it as well as I could before I finished dressing and went back to the dining room. The table was set with full plates of food: meats, pastries, eggs, everything I loved.

"Victoria, don't you have music lessons this morning?" I asked, waiting for Mother to join us before I started eating.

Victoria waved a nonchalant hand and shook her head. "I convinced my parents to let me skip them. You only turn sixteen once, you know."

"Well, it's been so long for you. Do you even remember what we did?" I snickered and dodged Victoria's well-aimed swat.

"Cyprus!" Mother chided, but she was well aware of my sense of humor.

"It's alright, Lady Reyner, I'm sure they accept returns at the shop where I purchased his gift," Victoria replied easily, turning up her nose at me.

"Victoria, you know you can call me Gwen. You're family here," Mother corrected her gently.

"I'm sorry, Gwen. It's…habit lately," Victoria replied.

"You didn't have to get me anything." Just knowing she'd skipped her lessons to spend time with me was more than enough. My mother finally took a seat and we began serving ourselves.

"I know I didn't. This year is something special, though. You'll have to be more kind than that if you want it, though." Victoria played the snobbish noble perfectly, but deep down I knew she'd always be the little girl sitting in the snow with me.

"Of course, my lady. Please, pardon my rudeness." I gave a little bow from my seat.

"Your father would have your hide if he saw you like this." Mother rolled her eyes, laughing as she did.

"Where is he, anyway?" I asked as I hastily shoveled food into my mouth.

"He couldn't find a replacement for his lecture today. But, he'll be joining us for dinner. Victoria, dear, of course, you're also welcome to join us."

"I'd love nothing more. We'll be back by then for certain," Victoria replied, taking dainty little bites of her breakfast. Everything she did was graceful and fluid. Often times I wondered how we'd become so close.

"Where are we going?" I asked. No one had told me there were plans for the day.

"It's a secret. You'll see." Victoria held one long finger against her lips and winked.

I may as well have inhaled the rest of breakfast. I wanted to know where Victoria was taking me and I didn't want to miss a second by her side. I waited what felt like years while she and my mother carried on idle conversation until finally Victoria collected a bundle beside her chair and stood.

"Always so impatient," she giggled and brushed her fingers through my hair.

"I didn't say anything!" I argued.

"You can't hide it from me." She turned to my mother. "Thank you for breakfast, Gwen. It was fantastic."

"Of course, dear. You're welcome here anytime."

"Thank you, Mother. See you for dinner?" I slipped on my boots.

"Yes, you two have fun, now." She waved us out the door with a hug and a kiss each.

The sun was still low on the horizon—I hadn't realized how early it was.

"How are you awake at this hour?" I stretched. Thanks to the large breakfast, I was ready to go back to bed.

"It isn't *that* early. Besides, I want to spend the whole day with you." She nudged me playfully.

The weather was pleasant and the city peaceful. Victoria led me by the hand past the houses and storefronts until we reached the trees.

"Now for a little adventure," she announced. This was the Victoria I'd always known— ready to take on the world. Afraid of nothing.

"Lead on, my lady." I bowed and she laughed. Her warm fingers weaved into mine and we made our way into the forest.

Soft moss gave way beneath our feet. The sun trickled through the pointed leaves and branches of the trees. Only a few easily scalable rocks threatened our path. The Istens surrounded us on either side as we climbed. By the time we reached our destination, the sun had cleared the horizon.

"I spent a lot of time looking for a spot just like this. I hope you like it," she said.

How could I not? She'd discovered a gap between the Istens where the Kingdom of Rhoryn spanned below us. We'd made our way above the clouds. Even so, we could see the distant outlines of the Capital's castle towers.

"Victoria, this is incredible," I breathed.

It was a spectacular view, one that gave me vertigo. When I turned back to her, she'd spread a blanket out on the soft ground and started to unpack the basket I'd helped carry.

"Good, because we'll be here for a while. Sit."

I obliged, taking a seat next to her. She unveiled two bottles of wine, finger foods and sandwiches, water, a pack of cards, and two wrapped bundles.

"I've never had wine before," I remarked, looking at the bottles.

"I know. This is a celebration that I think called for it." She smiled, handing me one of the wrapped bundles. "Gift number one."

Carefully untying the string, I unfolded the white cloth she'd used to cover the contents. Beneath it was a heavy, black fabric, lined with soft fur. I stood and held the edges so the rest of the fabric fell free.

"It's hard to get the both of us underneath one cloak, now. I thought you'd like one of your own." Despite our difference in age, I'd grown nearly a head taller than Victoria. She stood and swept it around my shoulders, latching it at the front. "Perfect fit."

It felt heavy and warm and wonderful. It reminded me of hers but lined with thicker fur. I adored it.

"Thank you, my lady." I gave it a flourish and she giggled. I sat beside her again and wrapped half of the cloak around her shoulders. With her petite frame, it comfortably fit us both.

"And gift the second," she murmured, pressing herself against me.

Everything about her made my head spin and I had to work hard to concentrate all of my focus on the second bundle. It was wrapped similarly and I quickly undid the knots. Inside were assorted quills, ink bottles, and a soft, leather-bound journal the color of Victoria's eyes.

"You have a talent for language…you should never give it up. I thought…I thought you may want somewhere more permanent than scraps of parchment to practice in."

It was a personal and generous gift. I couldn't imagine how much the journal alone had cost her.

She arranged the quills and ink bottles near the basket before reaching over to pull back the cover. "I thought I would start it off for you."

I love you. Three simple words were centered on the first page, written in Alavei, penned by Victoria's elegant hand. My heart raced and I was suddenly very aware of the heat of her skin against mine. The scent of her hair, the weight of her gaze. For so long I'd wondered why my entire being reacted so strongly to her. How to convey those feelings to her. How to tell her that I never wanted to leave her side. I would do anything for her. She'd said all that I wanted to in three little words.

"Cyprus, I…I'm sorry, it was silly—"

I pressed my lips to hers—my first kiss. Our first kiss. Her lips were so soft and welcoming.

"I love you, too," I murmured against her mouth.

She wrapped her arms around my neck and I slipped mine around her waist. I leaned back on the blanket and she followed, aligning her body to mine. My heart sang, my thoughts evaporated to nothing but her. She begged further exploration with her tongue and I parted my lips, breathless, eager to accept her request. Having never practiced, I could only attempt to reciprocate her motions. She moaned and fire surged through my veins. When she pulled away, I had trouble breathing. As if she had become the very source of my air and the absence of her choked me. I craved her. More of her. An empty wellspring deep inside of me had awakened and it was starving.

"Are you alright?" she whispered, brushing her fingertips down my neck. Her face was flushed.

I shuddered beneath her touch. "Gods, I…Yes. I've never been better," I breathed, drowning in the ocean of her eyes.

"You've never looked at me this way before."

"How's that?" I wanted to shift myself on top of her, taste every inch of her skin, draw more moans from her throat…*It's easy to lose yourself.*

"It's…intense," she struggled for the word, searching my face.

I had to restrain myself—we needed to stop before I did something I'd regret. "Nothing a little wine can't help?" I smiled and kissed her gently. "You did plan this whole day out, didn't you?"

She blushed and repositioned herself next to me, tugging on my cloak for me to sit up. Fishing a wine key from the basket, she poured the first two glasses of deep red liquid and handed me one. Taking her glass, she carefully touched it to mine.

"To many more namedays together," she toasted.

"Cheers to that."

"Just sip it. It'll take a bit to get used to," she instructed, taking a drink from her glass.

I did exactly that. The first drink was bitter and it was hard to hide my distaste. She laughed and handed me a piece of bread. I took a bite and tried again—this time it went down more smoothly, more flavors than "burning" danced across my tongue. By the third drink, my nerves had calmed and clear thoughts returned.

"It's not so bad," I teased her. "Surely better than the pisswater you drank on your sixteenth."

She burst out laughing. "I thought for sure you were going to tell your mother about that."

"That you, precious Victoria, bought enough cheap beer at the tavern to drown a horse? Because 'a lady never drinks,'" I quoted her father. "That I had to sober you up with an entire loaf of bread and listen to you sing lewd songs that you learned from heaven knows where for three hours?"

"It was *not* three hours," she refuted.

"Oh, my lady, it was three hours." I laughed and took another drink. "How did it go? 'Satins and silk, leathers and lace, the princess is locked up and all things but chaste?'"

"Cyprus Reyner, I did no such thing!" Her cheeks were bright red and she caught her breath between fits of laughter.

"Eventually, I joined in with you. Even if you don't remember. We made a pretty little harmony that I was sure would wake the city. I spent the entire next day convincing your parents something in the food made you sick. I don't know if they believed me, but somehow they still think you a lady."

"Perhaps I've become too good at pretending." She leaned her head against me and looked toward the castle.

"I don't think you're pretending," I replied, softening my tone. I wrapped my arm around her shoulders and pulled her close. "You're perfect the way you are."

We looked at the clouds for some time, enjoying each other's company. Eventually, we finished our first glass of wine and I moved to pour another as Victoria reached for the pack of playing cards she'd brought along.

"My uncle was by earlier this week, and he taught me a few games I thought you may enjoy." She tugged the cards from their casing.

"Is that so?" I watched her unpracticed fingers trip over the motions of shuffling the deck and smiled. My father was a card player and Victoria knew I was always on the lookout for new games to play with him.

"I thought we'd start with *Finan*."

She dealt the cards and we enjoyed the remainder of the evening learning new games and mastering them. Victoria wanted me to have a memorable sixteenth. It was one I would never forget.

IV

ictoria and I spent months hiding our affections for each other from our parents. I'm sure my mother knew very well what was happening, but I was terrified of what Madeline and Simon would think of me. If there was a place we could hide behind, my lips never left hers. If we were spared from supervision, Victoria's fingers wandered to my skin—beneath my tunic, tracing every inch she could manage before she was forced to stop. When I could no longer take the hours of teasing, I offered a few days' worth of translation work to the university library in exchange for a fair amount of coin. Enough for a good meal for Victoria and I…as well as a night at the inn.

In truth, I was terrified to tell Victoria of my idea. But when I finally managed the words, her excitement exceeded my expectations. I presented to my parents what I thought was a legitimate excuse for me to be out, but my mother saw right through me. She didn't say it outright, of course. However, the smile on her face said volumes when I told her I'd be gone for the evening. My father was confused, but she insisted it would be good for me as an adult.

I met Victoria at the only tavern and inn in Lorelyn after her daily lessons. We shared a hearty meal and drinks without worry, laughing and talking of her instructors and her true opinions of her lessons. When we finished our food and the drinks ran dry, both of us nervously eyed the stairs that led to the awaiting room.

"Think they'll let us take a bottle upstairs?" I asked in jest and she laughed. It eased the tension between us.

"No harm in asking, right?"

They did let us take a bottle with us. I took Victoria by the hand and guided her to the room I'd reserved for the night. My heart raced and my breathing was shallow. I unlocked the door to reveal a spacious area with a large bed and flowers on the nightstand. I placed the bottle carefully beside them and she shut the door, securing the latch. She ventured the few steps that lay between us and kissed me deeply. I hadn't expected her to initiate and it took me a moment to settle into her embrace. I wrapped my arms around her. She pressed her petite frame against my chest, urging me toward the bed.

"Victoria, wait." My heart was pounding against my chest and it took every ounce of resistance I had to move my hands to her shoulders. I had to work to clear my thoughts while she played at the ties on my tunic.

"Hmm?" Her eyes begged to know what was stopping me. I swallowed against the large lump that formed in my throat.

"If…if we do this…I'm afraid I'll accidentally hurt you," I admitted. Her cheeks were rose-colored from the wine. Her hair fell around her shoulders, framing her lovely face. I had to concentrate to keep my eyes from drifting lower.

"If I don't like something, I'll tell you to stop. Is that alright?" She made it sound so simple. Like there wasn't a latent instinct beneath my skin that wanted to consume her.

"I...alright," I replied.

Her mouth claimed mine and the ties of my shirt came loose. Her soft fingers drifted beneath, caressing my chest and throat. I moved to untie her corset strings, unbinding them within a few spans of our shared breathing. I maneuvered her onto the silken sheets and positioned myself on top of her.

"I love you," I whispered, kissing her cheek, then her throat.

"I love you, too," she gasped, her hands tugging my tunic over my head.

Every single nerve inside me was alive, fed by her hunger. My blood raced and boiled, begging for her to satiate my every desire. I pulled her shirt over her head. Victoria's pale skin contrasted perfectly against mine, her breasts flawlessly filled the frame of her torso. I dragged my mouth to her chest, using my tongue to tease and explore as much of her skin as I could manage. Every inch of her was beautiful. Her flesh tasted exactly as I'd imagined—sweet and delicate. Her quiet whimpers emboldened me, and I chanced to suck at her nipple. Her fingers entangled in my hair, and I succumbed to the heat of yearning that weaved through my veins. I traced her every contour, memorizing the map of her body with my fingertips, relishing in her moans and the sharp tugs at my hair. I moved my lips southward, tracing her ribs, her navel, her hips…

"Please," she breathed as I paused above her skirts. "Cyprus, don't stop."

"As you wish, my lady," I growled, pulling the thin fabrics down to her ankles.

I kissed her thigh, spreading her legs with my hands. All I knew was that I wanted to taste all of her. She'd promised to tell me if it was too much. I let my mouth drift between her legs—she gasped and pulled me harder against her by my hair. I parted her with my tongue and stroked the yielding folds of skin that lay beneath. My name escaped her lips and ecstasy washed over me.

"Higher…Like that," she moaned, guiding my movements.

I was more than pleased to comply. I would continue as long as she wanted me to. I drank her in and was intoxicated by her taste. I brushed my fingers across her thighs, across the perfect curve of her back, and grasped her hips, guiding her rhythmic movements to the speed I wanted. She arched her back in frustration, but it was a motion that only made me crave control. She was everything I'd ever wanted and more. The scent of her skin, the sounds of her moans, my name on her lips; I was dizzy with ecstasy. She pulled on my hair, bringing my mouth to hers in a deep, intimate kiss. Breathless, I pulled away for air.

"Can I…can I feel you?" Victoria begged, her eyes glancing to my trousers.

Her pleasure had taken precedence over my desires and I would have gladly spent the entire evening on her alone. Her request made my heart skip. I undid my belt with shaking hands. As soon as the latch was free, Victoria's hands joined mine in freeing me of my pants. I tossed them to the floor.

I repositioned myself on top of her, aligning my body to hers. She guided me to her with her fingers. I gasped as I slowly entered her—she was tight, soaked with pleasure, and scorching with need. When my hips met hers, her cries of desperation nearly brought me over the edge. She felt incredible. Even the slight twitches of her body took their toll on my fortitude. I bent and kissed her, exploring the whole of her mouth with my tongue. My hands wandered the landscape of her skin. I allowed her to set the pace despite my craving for control.

"I'm sorry…I'm really close," I murmured against her lips.

"Then let go," she instructed, her eyes meeting mine. Her piercing gaze pushed me past my breaking point.

I thrust into her as deep as her body allowed—every aspect of her sent me into delirium. As I set a new, faster rhythm, cries of delight took hold of her and she wrapped her legs around me. She closed her eyes and she moved her hands from my hair to grasp the bars in the headboard. Her entire body clenched and I felt the first waves of release wash over me, sounds I didn't recognize tore from my throat. My fingers tangled in her hair, tongue deep in her throat, I plunged through her climax until I was breathless. When I slowed, we gasped for air in unison. Clear thoughts returned to me and for a moment and I panicked.

"Victoria, I didn't hurt you, did I?"

"No." She smiled. "Quite the opposite, actually."

I drew away from her and lay to her side. I wrapped my arms around her and pulled her in.

"Did...did you like it?" Confidence evaded me—the last thing I wanted was to disappoint her. "I'm sorry I couldn't hold out longer."

"Cyprus, that was amazing. Hush." She laughed, moving her hands to my face.

I found myself drowning in the depths of her eyes. "You're so beautiful."

She blushed and tucked her head beneath my chin. "I love you."

"I love you, too." I kissed her forehead and held her against me. The warmth of her skin against mine lulled me to sleep.

I wish we could have stayed like that forever.

V

The university begged me to stay full-time after I finished my few days of translating for them. Wanting a source of income to put toward Victoria and my evenings alone, I agreed and worked for them in the mornings. My parents were more than happy to see me harness such a drive for learning—especially my father. Even if they didn't realize my motivations for doing so.

My mother was right to advise me of what to expect of myself. After the first night Victoria and I spent together, I thought of nothing else. I craved her as a basic need—her touch, her taste, her body, her voice. Our shared evenings at the inn grew more passionate the more we explored each other. The anticipation of each new encounter became my reason for living.

I began to stash away extra gold from my weekly income. I wanted to save for a ring to ask Victoria to be by my side for eternity. I didn't want something in the typical fashion of Lorelyn, but a piece that symbolized her and me together as a pair. The jeweler in Lorelyn would already charge an arm for what I wanted. But, for a Whisper? Most likely double.

So I worked tirelessly for two years until I hoped I'd saved enough to commission the ring I dreamed of. Thankfully, I had more than I needed. I learned that the jeweler himself was a member of the university and wouldn't dare overcharge me.

I requested a ring of white, and the jeweler insisted he'd created an alloy of gold that turned white in the process—already setting it apart from the traditional rings I saw most of the ladies of Lorelyn wear. I asked for various gemstones—one that would celebrate our namedays, the colors of winter, the hues of love. The jeweler only laughed and told me he knew exactly what I was looking for.

One fateful day, when Victoria and I were both free of studies and work obligations, we perused the stalls of Lorelyn. It wasn't often that we shared a day in the city—we spent most of our free hours with each other alone, or with prior responsibilities. We were browsing a well-respected wine store when a man approached Victoria.

"Excuse me, my lady. I'm afraid I've lost my way." He spoke in perfect Alavei. "Though, it seems the heavens have sent me an angel to guide me."

Victoria laughed. My defenses raised but, really, he'd done nothing wrong. Victoria was stunningly beautiful. It wasn't the first time that she received such compliments.

"And where are you trying to go, my lord?" she replied, the thick accent of Reln painting her words. She hadn't perfected the dialect as I had, but I found it endearing.

"The apothecary. I'm a physician, you see. I've heard tales of Lorelyn-made cures the likes of which the rest of Rhoryn has never seen." He offered his hand and she took it.

Hints of jealousy simmered inside of me as he brushed her knuckles with his lips. I wondered how he'd caught her attention so easily—there were plenty of people who visited Lorelyn that she never spared a second glance.

"You almost made it, lord…"

"Jeremi Terryn, if it would please my lady."

Victoria turned to me. "Do you mind if I show him?"

"No, go ahead," I replied. I didn't want to seem weak or jealous.

He was tall and striking, held a prestigious position…But I loved Victoria and she constantly reciprocated my affections. Nothing should have bothered me about the encounter. So what had my stomach in knots?

"This way, Jeremi," she announced, linking her arm through his and leading him out the door.

I purchased two bottles we hadn't tried and waited outside the shop for Victoria to return.

Seconds dragged on like years. She returned in good time, taking my hand without a care in the world. She acted as if she'd already forgotten about Jeremi Terryn, leading me toward the inn and chattering excitedly about the new patterns she'd learned to sew. I put Lord Terryn out of my mind, once again enjoying her company.

I was a fool.

A week following our acquisition of new wine and another evening spent together, there was a knock on my door. Victoria hadn't made an appearance since that day—not uncommon for her—and I knew she had lessons that morning. My mother and I were both surprised to see Simon d'Audrieu standing on our doorstep.

"Pardon my intrusion, Lady Reyner, but may I speak with Cyprus?" I was standing right beside my mother and wondered why he addressed her first.

"Of course, m'lord," I replied, grabbing my cloak from beside the door.

My mother remained silent as I joined Simon outside.

"I'll be back in a little while," I assured her.

"Of course, sweet," she responded, closing the door behind me.

Simon led the way, letting the uncomfortable silence linger between us for as long as possible. After what felt like an eternity, we reached the collection of trees that Victoria and I had claimed as our own so many years before. I wondered if he knew its significance.

"Cyprus, there comes a time in a man's life when he has to choose between what he wants, and what is best," he began. The tone he used was one I associated with my father when he was lecturing me.

I didn't care for it. "What are you talking about, Master d'Audrieu?" Whatever he was trying to get to, he was dancing around it and I didn't have time for niceties.

"I know what Victoria means to you and I understand this will be hard to hear. But it's time you thought of what is truly the right path for her," he explained calmly, avoiding my gaze.

"And what is the *right* path for her?" I saw where the conversation was going. My emotions tainted the words spilling from my mouth.

"Well, between a Whisper whose final resting place lies in Lorelyn and a physician that can show her the world she's always dreamed of…Cyprus, do you see what I'm getting at?"

"And how did you meet Jeremi Terryn?" I couldn't believe what I was hearing. Victoria would have never offered us as an option to her father—he'd never cared for me.

"He brought us dinner the evening after Victoria guided him through Lorelyn. He's…quite taken with her, Cyprus. They've spent nearly every moment together this past week. He's offered her everything she's ever wanted."

In my selfish train of thought, I had to bite my tongue. *But I'm all that she's ever wanted.* I knew I wasn't. I watched her look over the Istens every time we were together, wondering what life was like in Anastas, in Valford, in the Capital. Her heart existed outside the walls of Lorelyn, and with my status and savings, I couldn't give it to her.

"As a plea from a Father for his daughter, Cyprus, I just want you to consider the situation. I understand how hard this is for you, but please, she's waited all her life for an opportunity like this one," he explained.

I couldn't bring myself to say anything to Simon. My reality was crumbling. I knew exactly what he was asking for and I knew she would want the same thing. She would be torn, of course. It would tear her apart more than any decision had in her life. And it all hinged on me. My feelings, my desires. I was aware of my intentions, but hers were divided.

"I appreciate your concern, Simon. It's something I'll have to think on," I said as calmly as I could manage.

He put a hand on my shoulder as if he surmised that I was falling apart. "Thank you for taking Victoria's future into consideration."

I nodded and watched him go. I buried every sound and word that threatened to tear from my throat. I buried my fist into one of the nearby trees.

I needed to see the jeweler.

That night, I sat beneath our tree unable to sleep. To my surprise Victoria joined me, folding her cloak beneath her to sit next to me. We looked toward the Istens in silence for a long time, neither of us knowing what subject was safe to broach.

"Jeremi...he brought my family an entire dinner for showing him to the apothecary," she began.

I nodded my reply. The fresh wounds on my knuckles were just beginning to scab over. I felt disconnected from the pain.

"He said...he said he's visiting from Anastas. That he's been looking for medicines like ours for a long time...He's told me so many incredible stories over the past week...Promised me so many things..."

"Come here." I wrapped my cloak around her shoulders, pulling her into me as she had done more than a decade before. I kissed her forehead and she leaned against me. Her father's words ran through my head without reprieve. She was clearly torn and I had to make the decision to let her go. "I made you a promise a long time ago."

"Cyprus," I could hear the tears choking her speech.

"I told you I would lead you to your prince, didn't I?" She deserved her happy ending. It wasn't with me in Lorelyn.

"But I...we..." Her tears dampened my shirt.

I held back cries of my own. "I will always love you." I retrieved the small box from my pocket. "But you deserve a better life than this."

She took the box with her delicate hands, opening it to reveal the ring I'd waited so long to give her. The ring that symbolized everything that we were. I'd added one final touch.

"This is beautiful…I can't accept this—"

"It's yours. It was made for you." I slipped it onto her delicate hand. A perfect fit—I'd made sure of it. "On the inside, there's an engraving. It says *Tere L'etai*."

"Love Freely?"

"A Whispers creed, my love. Perhaps one that you could also benefit from."

"How?"

"Just…love with all your heart. No matter why or whom or when. Love with everything you have."

She glanced at the ring in the shimmering moonlight before her arms surrounded my waist and she buried her face in my chest.

"Cyprus…I don't want to leave you," she cried.

"I'll always be here, I promise." I barely recognized my own voice. I wanted to cry with her, to tell her that I was lying—I could hardly breathe without her. "This is…this is your chance to fly."

We stayed in each other's arms until the sun rose.

The next morning, Victoria left with Jeremi Terryn for Anastas.

VI

espite Victoria's absence, her letters flowed in like the storms of winter. For months I read them and didn't respond, unsure of what I could say to not harm our fragile relationship. Eventually, I gave in and responded to her missives—my last link to the woman I loved so dearly. I moved to a small home of my own, not wanting to bother my parents with my state of affairs.

My mother fretted about me constantly, knowing what it had cost me to surrender the one I cared for most to another man. I assured her I was fine, but in truth, I wasn't.

On top of the emotional turmoil that ravaged me every single day, the physical desires that screamed through my veins were enough to send me to the brink of insanity. I dreamed of Victoria's eyes, touch, moans, and lips. More often than not, I woke up shaking with need. Despite longing gazes from the ladies of Lorelyn, I wasn't ready to share the bed of another. So I suppressed my urges, attempting to ignore my very nature.

I kept my position at the university, hoping that one day I would make enough to move my life to another city—away from my memories.

Shortly after Jeremi and Victoria married, one of the letters she sent me proposed that I accept a position as their Ring. I'd never heard of such a thing, but in Anastas, there were temples that initiated the ceremony. A third person would join an established couple, essentially like a marriage but as an equal lover to both parties. I thought of Jeremi's hands on Victoria's ivory skin, his mouth on hers. I respectfully declined.

One afternoon while I worked on translating a new manuscript, a man my age approached me. I glanced up from my task in time to see him set a stack of books on the table.

"What can I do for you, sir?" I asked curiously, looking over the tomes he'd brought along.

"I've heard you're the one to come to about translations into Alavei." He brushed his dark hair away from his face and smiled easily. "I'm a little rusty and could use the practice. I'm Kaelin Ligas, by the way."

"Cyprus Reyner. Well met." I took a page from Victoria's book. I shook his hand and returned his smile.

"I'd like to pay you to teach me if you don't mind."

"Not at all, have a seat."

We spent hours together—teaching him was a welcome distraction and the extra income would help me with my aspirations of leaving.

When the sun set and the university closed, Kaelin invited me to his home to have dinner with him and his wife. I reluctantly accepted, my only other option wallowing at home by myself.

They lived in a large estate, obviously funded by the wealth of Kaelin's land ownership. Elaina Ligas was a treasure—funny, witty, and clever. She matched wits with her husband and me, and we had a wonderful time laughing over supper. They both invited me back the following evening and the next. I continued to teach Kaelin Alavei and my visits with them alleviated some of the painful loneliness that haunted me.

After a few weeks, I brought three bottles of wine and was feasting with them when they proposed something that made my heart skip a beat.

"Cyprus…would you like to stay with us for the evening?" It was Kaelin who offered.

Of course, I knew what he was asking. I didn't know how to respond. Every craving in my body said yes, every emotion in my heart said no. But Victoria was out of my reach. Why was I denying myself my base outlet?

"I'd like that very much." I set my glass down and leaned back into my seat. I was afraid to assume. "Is there a guest room I should make myself comfortable in?"

"No…we'd like you to sleep in our bed," Elaina replied, then immediately blushed. "I mean, if you're not comfortable, it's alright—"

I laughed. "I didn't want to presume, my lady. Yes, it's alright."

She stood and Kaelin followed her lead. I watched them both, interested in what they had planned. Elaina took my hand and led me to their chambers, Kaelin close behind. When we arrived, my heart was already racing, blood pounding in my ears. The dormant thirst that lay within me came pouring out—there was nothing to hold me back. I had Elaina's clothes off in seconds, and they had mine in mere moments following. Elaina and I both stripped Kaelin of his garments and the three of us stood bare to each other. I needed to feel naked skin against mine with the desperation of a man starved. My lips met Elaina's, Kaelin's mouth was at my ear. The feeling of two people was overwhelming—they enveloped me and I succumbed to their wills.

All three of us went to the floor, the soft carpet rubbing against my knees—me on top of Elaina, Kaelin behind me. I thrust into Elaina, her cries matching mine. I muffled them against her throat as Kaelin bit my shoulder. He drove inside me and my body immediately reacted. I pushed back against his hips. Elaina followed suit, bringing her hips up to mine, forcing Kaelin deeper into me. A few seconds of pain gave way to a pleasure I'd never experienced and I couldn't repress the moans that tore from my throat. They unknowingly imprinted an entirely new level of ecstasy into me. I craved more.

I plunged my tongue deep into Elaina's throat, exploring every inch of her mouth. She quivered and her nails dug into my back. I lifted my head and Kaelin's mouth claimed hers.

Between the tight fit of Elaina and Kaelin's hungry rhythm, I couldn't hold back my orgasm. I didn't want to hold back. My body went rigid in climax, pleasure dancing across my spine. They each moved independently and dragged it out as long as they could. I cried out as they continued bucking and thrusting against me.

"You're not done," Kaelin advised, his breath hot in my ear.

He was right, I wasn't. Despite my panting, shuddering form, all I could think about was more. They'd unleashed the raw lust I'd suppressed for so long.

"We'll see how far you can go." Elaina flashed a wicked smile, her apprehensive demeanor completely vanished.

She kissed me as she squirmed out from beneath me. While she was occupied, Kaelin repositioned me on my back and his lips met mine. His kiss was rough and carnal, accentuated with teasing nips. Elaina returned shortly after, holding a long measure of rope.

"Let's see how you do while bound, hmm?" She knelt by my head, running her fingers through my hair.

Kaelin guided my arms above my head and Elaina went to work, tying intricate knots that only tightened when struggled against.

I let them do anything they wanted with me. And I drank in every second of it.

I spent months in their care, forcing myself beyond limits I thought were possible. Each time I thought we'd explored every sexual facet possible, they thought of something new to try. Elaina taught me her knots and I found gratification in binding them both.

They'd also heard of the Rings Victoria had mentioned. They wanted so desperately for me to join them as one. I agreed not long after they asked and followed through with the ceremony. We found a small residence that performed the official ceremony within Lorelyn for an exorbitant fee. They paid for it without hesitation. The tattoo on my finger stung for weeks, but I somehow convinced myself that it was the right thing to do.

Many evenings I found myself awake and sleepless, reading Victoria's letters. The Ligas' filled a little piece of the void she'd left in my heart, but hearing from her remained the highlight of my days.

I was their Ring for six years, sharing in their joys, their pains, and their pleasures. It was everything my body desired and nothing my heart ever asked for. Our relationship held fast.

Until Elaina questioned the vows we all stood for.

"I'm afraid I'm losing you to him," I overheard her saying to Kaelin one day. "We're husband and wife—doesn't that mean anything to you?"

"Elaina, you're over thinking this—"

"You don't look at me the same way as you used to. You don't treat me the same way. It's him or me, Kaelin."

It was laughable, really, for her to think I'd want to take her husband away from her. When in reality, everything I wanted existed only in Anastas.

I didn't tell either of them of my departure—I thought it better that way. I simply packed my things and returned to my parents' home where they accepted me with open arms. I needed time to think, time to reconsider my options. I had plenty of money saved to move wherever I wanted. But, what I truly wanted wasn't possible.

Unfortunately, after three years of consideration, the decision was made for me.

VII

pon your death, your father came to my door. Filled with empty apologies and hollow regrets, he told me you and Jeremi were murdered. He told me they couldn't read the will without my presence. I must admit, I could care less about the will.

I holed myself in my house until Madeline came to drag me out. Your mother, the one who told you to be wary of Whispers, stood in my doorway and told me how much you loved me. That if you were still here, you wouldn't be able to stand seeing me like this. She was right—you wanted adventure, exploration, something new. For both of us. Who was I to deny your final wishes?

In nearly every other letter, you mentioned a tavern you often frequented with Jeremi and your Ring. The Cursed Elixir—a strange name for a place to cure one of their sorrows and ailments. Regardless, I stood at the wooden door, wondering if I'd be accepted as your family had been. Once, you must have stood on these very steps, right Victoria?

I made my way through the door to find it crowded and noisy—but not unpleasant. An older, built-to-last woman bustled between tables, taming the patrons who pestered her and serving those patient enough to wait for their food. I surveyed my current landscape, wondering where a Whisper could fit in.

And, that's when....That's when I saw her.

Victoria, she was beautiful—you chose well.

Josselyn sat in a booth by herself, her eyes focused on something unseen, her fingers wrapped around the stem of a wine glass. She was a Whisper, just like me. Just as you'd said. Every rumor surrounding her painted her as your murderer and upon seeing her face, I was torn. Our race was judged immediately—as my mother constantly reminded me—however, the motive for her to dispatch the both of you was still there.

I stood in the door until the intimidating barmaid approached me.

"What can I do you for?" she asked, not unkind, holding her hand out to take my cloak.

"I...I think I'll take a seat on my own. Thank you," I replied, glancing at Josselyn's table.

She followed my eyes and nodded. "Just don't cause trouble, alright?" Without another word, she took my cloak and left, returning to the tables that beckoned for her.

You'd entrusted everything to her. Laid your hopes and dreams in her. But why? What had it gained you?

My only option was to speak with Josselyn and pray that your trust was not misplaced. I made my way to her table, running through so many words that I could say to her. I could only come up with something I thought amusing.

"Well, well. What have we here? A wisp in Anastas?" I leaned against Josselyn's table.

Her face went from confused to defiant in a matter of seconds before meeting my eyes.

Victoria…I see why you loved her so desperately. Just in her astonished gaze, I wanted to lose myself.

Josselyn Thorn may be the death of me.

REMEMBER

BOOK TWO
OF
WHISPERS FROM THE PAST

I

It was the first time I'd ever smelled salt in the air. Seen an expanse of water that continued infinitely. A warm, steady breeze played at my hair, caressed my skin. The ocean mirrored the full moon, illuminating the picturesque scene before me. If it weren't for the circumstances surrounding our visit, the City of Ends was easily one of the most stunning landscapes I'd ever seen.

"Victoria, love. I…don't how to prepare you for this." Jeremi's fingers weaved into mine.

"I'm the one who asked to come here. I want to understand every part of your life. This weight…you should not have to bear it alone." I met his gaze and smiled—the waves danced in his silver eyes.

"I don't know what I've ever done to deserve you." He sighed and kissed my hair.

I leaned into him. "Your actions answer that every day, my sweet. Nothing I see here will change how I see you."

I inhaled the perfumed air one last time before hooking my arm through his. Delaying the inevitable would lead us nowhere.

"Shall we go?" I asked.

"Alright," he replied reluctantly.

We turned and made our way back into the heart of the city. It was alive with food, trade, and music. Despite the joyous atmosphere, the City of Ends was well known for its black market and underhanded business dealings. The location couldn't be better—far enough from the Capital that most lawmen didn't bother to visit unless doing business themselves and close enough to the ocean to encourage trade by sea.

Jeremi kept me close, weaving through inebriated citizens, dealers hawking their wares, and the occasional courtesan who reconsidered their propositions to my husband upon meeting my gaze. We stopped in front of a large, unmarked building built against an enormous cliff. Two giant men flanked the doorway in religious garb, their forms illuminated only by a single lantern that hung above the threshold. They shifted position to block our entry as we approached.

"I'm sorry, m'lord. There's a service currently in session," said the one at the right, his voice low and rough.

"We've come to pay our respects," Jeremi replied easily, bowing his head.

I copied his movements, though my heart pounded against my chest.

"Do you believe the gods to favour you?" the one on the left asked.

"No, sir, the gods favour fortune," Jeremi said as if reciting a prayer.

"You may enter," they replied simultaneously, stepping aside.

Jeremi led, taking my hand and pushing open the heavy wooden door.

It took a moment for my eyes to adjust to the dim lighting and I followed Jeremi blindly into the crowd. The walls were bare, spare a few torches for light, and the floor was made of solid stone. We were surrounded by people dressed in expensive clothing and heavily coated in perfumes. When we found an open place to stand, a maiden in a daringly low corset and slit skirt approached to ask if we would like something to drink. I considered the liquid courage but quickly declined—I needed to witness this sober. Chatter of job dealings, land holdings, and estate matters filled the room and I could barely hear my own thoughts. At the head of the room—the best lit area of it all—was a raised platform. Almost like a performer's stage. I stared at it curiously when Jeremi's voice was at my ear.

"If you need to leave, don't hesitate, I'll follow you. Understand?"

I nodded my reply. My heart hadn't slowed, my mouth was parched. Could I really stand by and watch this?

"Victoria—" Jeremi began but never finished.

"Good evening, ladies and gentlemen." A pulchritudinous man dressed in lavish clothing addressed the crowd from the platform.

Silence immediately befell the room and all attention turned to him.

"Thank you for joining us for tonight's auction. I'm pleased to announce we have an exceptional lineup available for purchase. If this is your first time attending, there are a few bidding rules to address. Please keep your bids at a minimum increase of one hundred gold, only make bids you intend to pay, and be prepared to read and sign the house's contract upon your purchase. Failure to follow these rules will lead to a permanent ban from the auction house. Let's begin with lot one."

A man the same size as the giants standing guard at the door appeared from behind the auctioneer. He tugged at a chain that led to a short, fragile boy who couldn't have been older than ten. Wearing nothing but a thin pair of shorts, his stomach curved dangerously inward as if he hadn't eaten in weeks. His hands were bound behind him, and his shackled feet dragged across the floor until he stopped on the platform. His shoulders slumped, eyes blank, fair hair covered in dirt—this was a broken child. Jeremi's hand tightened around my own and I bit my lip to hold back from gasping.

"Lot one comes to us from Maura, sold to the City of Ends after the sudden death of his parents. He is in fair health and responds well to training. Bidding starts at two hundred gold."

Murmurs spread around the room and I felt dizzy listening to their questions. Boys were apparently not often seen and highly sought after for a multitude of reasons.

"Who would like to start us off?" The auctioneer interrupted the hum of voices.

"Three hundred!" a man cried from the crowd.

"Four hundred!" shouted another woman.

The bidding continued until it reached two thousand gold. It was an amount that, for someone of my lineage, would have fed my family for months.

A hush fell across the room, the boy's gaze lulled to the floor.

"Two thousand gold. Going once? Twice? Thrice? Sold, to the lovely woman in the back, there. Congratulations! Please make your way to the escritoire to complete your purchase."

There was a light round of applause as the boy was pulled off the stage toward his new life. I prayed she would at least give him a decent meal. But from what Jeremi had informed me happens to many of those auctioned, I feared the worst.

The auction continued, the same ritual repeated for each person. Not a name was announced; simply their lot number, origin, state of health, perhaps something interesting picked up from the selling party, and their starting bid.

Jeremi had done his best to explain to me exactly how his family's business worked. Why he'd abandoned the Markov name in favor of Terryn, that of all the shady dealings in the City of Ends it was by far the worst. Even so, the casual way the crowd spoke of prices, the perfunctory comments made in relation to appearance or physique, and the vulgar obscenities that some men whispered behind their accompanying female companions—those were the things that he could have never prepared me for.

It wasn't long before I realized I *couldn't* stand and watch. I turned to lead us both away from the horrors of the auction house.

"Lot seven comes to us from Veritas. Sold to the City of Ends by her parents for much-needed funds. She is in good health. Please be perfectly sure of your bids, as lot seven is a Whisper."

I froze mid-stride and my heart skipped a beat. Turning once more to the auction stage, the guard led a girl—she was so young—to the platform. Her white hair was blackened with filth, her tanned skin was scored and bruised. They'd stripped her naked, bound her tighter than any despite her lack of resistance, and pushed her to her knees on the platform.

"Bidding starts at four thousand gold coins."

The muttering escalated to a dull roar. A Whisper? Had anyone ever seen a Whisper before? Was it true, the rumors, about them…you know?

"Jeremi," I whimpered, clutching his sleeve. I hadn't realized I'd ceased breathing. The bids were out of control, jumping from the thousands to the tens of thousands in under a minute.

"Adrien can't know we're here—"

"Please, love," I begged, "you of all people know what will happen to her if it's anyone else. We can't…We can't leave her." Memories raced in place of my consciousness—Cyprus teaching me Alavei, his face the first time he tried wine, the sound of his heartbeat. *Tere L'etai.*

"Victoria—"

"Please," I whispered. The tears I'd stifled throughout the ordeal flowed free. "Jeremi, I'll do anything."

He kissed the tears that lingered on my cheeks. "You've already given me everything."

"Forty thousand gold coins. Going once?" The auctioneer announced.

"Forty-five thousand!" Jeremi declared.

"Forty-six thousand!" another man from across the room responded.

"Fifty thousand gold!" Jeremi's bid silenced the room.

I was sure they could all hear my heart pounding.

"Fifty thousand gold. Going once? Twice? Thrice?"

I held my breath.

"Sold, to the gentleman to my right! Congratulations! Please make your way to the escritoire to complete your purchase!"

That was the first night Josselyn Thorn spent in our care.

II

In Jeremi's estate, only a select few trusted servants worked beneath him. While I liked them well enough, I couldn't be sure of their reactions to Josselyn. Upon our hasty return, I drew her a bath myself. She hadn't so much as uttered a word in our presence, her name we gleaned from the contract.

Now she huddled in Jeremi's cloak on the floor of the bedroom, watching me intently while I filled the tub with hot water and a few drops of scented oils. I rolled up my sleeves and offered my hand to her. She stared at it warily.

"What...what will you do with me?" Josselyn's first words to me were laced with terror. Her voice shook and she hastily retreated from my extended arm.

"Well, my dear, I thought you might enjoy a bath first." I sat down on the floor across from her, keeping the same distance between us. "I'm sure we can find something for you to wear while you eat and rest. After that, we'll see how you feel. How does that sound?"

"Please don't t-touch—um," she stammered, drawing her knees in close to her chest. She refused to meet my gaze.

"Don't what?"

"I...I'm sure you've heard things...about Whispers. But I don't like it when..." she trailed off as tears streamed down her face. "I don't like it…" Her fingers clutched Jeremi's cloak so tightly to her body that her knuckles turned white.

My heart shattered. "Oh, sweetheart. No, nothing like that will happen here." I was so concerned with her life after the auction that I'd never stopped to consider what may have transpired before.

"They…all of them, they…" Her words choked on sobs. She loosened her grip on the cloak and covered her face with her hands. "I never wanted any of it…"

I couldn't let her feel isolated. As if what she'd endured meant nothing. I moved slowly—as not to frighten her—and wrapped my arms around her small frame. "You're safe now, Josselyn. I promise you."

She buried her face against my chest and cried—misery wracked and shook her entire body. I held her close and murmured sweet nothings into her hair.

At a very young age, my parents had advised me to stay away from Whispers. In truth—we were the monsters who never considered their humanity.

As Josselyn's weeping quieted, she leaned back to look up at me. I wiped the remaining tears from her face and smiled.

"I don't even know your names." She laughed wryly.

"Victoria Terryn. My husband is Jeremi Terryn. Welcome home, Josselyn."

I found myself peeking—for the hundredth time that night—into the guest room where Josselyn slept soundly.

After her bath, Jeremi, and I grabbed as many different kinds of food items as possible and presented them to her, letting her pick at whatever she wanted. We surmised that since we didn't know what she liked, it was better to have a selection. Josselyn ate a little bit of everything, stuffing herself near to bursting.

Once her hunger was satiated, she timidly remarked that she hadn't realized how much her back hurt. I suggest Jeremi take a look at it but immediately retracted my statement when panic flooded her features. Jeremi noticed her fear as well and quickly suggested a tincture to help her sleep that would dull the pain. We hoped she was comfortable enough in the morning to at least let Jeremi examine her back.

"Can't sleep?" Jeremi weaved his arms around my waist. His lips brushed my shoulder.

"Jeremi, what they did to her is unforgivable," I murmured, leaning into his embrace.

"The bastards Adrien has handling these people are paid little and care less." He sighed.

"Have you never tried to put an end to it?"

"Their system of business is so fail-safe that even as the brother of the man running it, I can't take it down. I've wanted nothing more, ever since I was a boy," he admitted. "I...studied medicine in the hopes of helping more people than Adrien could hurt."

Each choice Jeremi made in his life was focused on assisting others. He was tender, gentle, and kind. I fell more in love with him every day.

"She's only thirteen. I'm terrified that she'll be forced to carry an illegitimate child from one of those mongrels," I confessed.

"Victoria...Female Whispers can't have children."

"...What?" I asked, abashed. "Why not?"

"It's something in their heritage. Unexplained. I've treated a few female Whisper patients and it's all the same—none of them were able to conceive."

"So she'll...she'll never have the *choice* of being a mother?"

"No, she won't." He kissed the top of my head. "And time will only tell if her parents told her as much."

I watched the steady rise and fall of her chest, the peaceful look on her face. Josselyn was born deprived of a basic, feminine instinct. As a mere teen, her innocence was stolen from her and her childhood rendered forfeit. I held back tears.

"What can we do for her?" I was at a loss. "How do we...fix this?"

"I don't know, love. But we'll do everything we can to try." Jeremi squeezed me tight. "Of that, I can promise you."

The world was an exquisite, volatile place—for so long I'd yearned to comb every inch. Jeremi had shown me incredible sights; from the City of Ends to the furthest reaches of Rhoryn. Even so, my greatest adventure lay in offering a second chance to a young Whisper who'd never been afforded a first. Jeremi led me back to bed where I slept soundly for the rest of the evening.

III

here were nights when I'd wake in darkness to hear Josselyn crying out in pain. I'd rush to her side to calm her—her sheets drenched in sweat and tears streaking her face. For a time they were so frequent that I took up to reading her fairy tales—anything to get her poor, tortured mind off of the demons that plagued her. She adored them. Some nights we would read them before she slept. Eventually, her cries stopped completely and I think all three of us felt better for it.

One afternoon, I was tending to my gardens when Josselyn appeared by my side.

"These are beautiful," she commented, her voice quiet and cautious.

"Thank you." I smiled, continuing to water each flower and trim to the leaves with care.

"What…um…what are all of these flowers called?" She rested beside me, intently looking over each plant.

"Well, here we have amaranth, daisies, marigolds, and…" I struggled on the last flower. I could only think of the name I'd called them in Lorelyn. "…*Elsine.*"

"*Elsine?*" The word rolled off her tongue awkwardly and I smiled, finally remembering the name of the delicate white flower.

"Lilies. They're lilies." I corrected myself, stroking the petals.

"My lady—"

"Victoria, sweet. No need for formalities."

"Why did you and Jeremi choose me? From…from the auction?"

My breathing caught and my mind stumbled over the things I could say to her. I didn't want to explain to her that she reminded me of Cyprus, someone I loved dearly—it may only serve to plant a seed of doubt in her perceptions of me. I left one Whisper behind, why not another? I couldn't say it was because of her physical traits—clearly, she was already familiar with the talents Whispers were rumored to harness. I couldn't tell her it was because Jeremi's family owned the business—what kind of faith would that place in Jeremi?

"We both understood what would happen if we didn't. I've…heard the rumors about Whispers, just as you've suggested. And truly, only you should be able to decide if and when those feelings happen."

"I see…I'm glad you decided to…to purchase me."

"Josselyn—"

"How do you decide who to love?" Josselyn's small fingers traced the petals of a daisy.

I paused. Her mind was reeling but I wanted to grant her the most honest answers possible. "Most times, sweet, you don't *decide* who to love. Love just…happens."

We were silent for a time. Josselyn caressed the delicate flowers while I watered them.

"Do you mind if I help you with your garden more often? I'd like to learn how," she requested.

"Of course, Josselyn. I'd love your assistance." I smiled.

We started with the basics of watering and upkeep. I promised to show her planting and growing techniques in the following weeks. She was an attentive student and I enjoyed teaching her.

A few days following Josselyn's first lessons in the gardens, I found her and Jeremi beneath the gazebo near our estate. I'd requested it built to spend time reading outside amongst the gardens and Jeremi had it done within days. His hand guided hers with a quill in smooth strokes on a piece of parchment as he spelled out the letters.

"J-o-s-s-e-l-y-n. See? Josselyn. That's your name," he said.

"It looks…pretty, like that," she replied in awe.

"Now you try."

"J…o…s…s…l?" she giggled and moved to the next line, starting her name over.

Jeremi was immensely patient with her—perhaps a better teacher at language than I was at gardening. But seeing Josselyn at her leisure with him lifted a great weight from my heart.

It wasn't long before we renovated the guest room to be Josselyn's permanent chambers. We changed the colors to ones she fancied, added a large bookcase and chess set—a game Jeremi adored playing with her. When we presented her with the new furnishings, she gifted each of us with a hug before touching every piece of fabric and material we'd added. Her embrace marked the first of many and the first glimpses of her trust in us both.

"Jeremi said you know another language besides Alavei," Josselyn commented as she helped me plant a new section of lilies.

"Yes. I know Reln," I replied simply. I wiped a line of sweat from my brow with my forearm.

"Where did you learn that?"

"From Lorelyn, where I grew up. I know Reln much better than I know Alavei. For example...*elsine*." I pointed to the lilies.

"Oh! That's Reln! El-si-nay..." she pronounced slowly.

I knew I had an accent when I spoke Alavei—Jeremi thought it was "adorable." It was much heavier than Cyprus' minor lilt of his words. He'd perfected it in a way I never thought possible. Remembering our studies together, I self-consciously toyed at the ring he'd given me. "Josselyn, have you ever heard the phrase *Tere L'etai?*"

"…No," she replied after a moment, letting soil seep through her fingers.

"It's the creed of a Whisper. It translates to *Love Freely.* I wish I could explain it a little better, but…I think I'm beginning to learn what it means."

"What's that?"

"No matter what happens, no matter how much you feel you're hurt or lost, love with all of your heart. Hold nothing back."

She nodded and looked up at me, her blue eyes more alive and bright than I'd ever seen them. "I…I think I understand."

Turning her focus back to the flowers, she leaned against me. It was the first time she'd touched her skin to mine. I smiled and shifted the attentions of her hands to another flower.

Two weeks before her sixteenth nameday, I found Josselyn and Jeremi in her room, mulling over a game of chess. Jeremi was surely winning, but giving her the chance to get back at him. I'd never understood the finer points of the game and enjoyed watching them play. Josselyn held her concentration and I observed them quietly from the doorway. Her chin rested in the palm of her hand as she bit her nails out of thoughtful habit. After a few passes of the board with her eyes, she picked up a piece and placed it further in.

"Check." She smiled proudly.

When her gaze lifted from the board, I saw something in how she looked at Jeremi. A heat I'd always associated with Cyprus.

"And how will you respond, my love?" I approached Jeremi and weaved my arms around his neck.

When Josselyn shifted her attentions to mine, I'd expected the fire to disappear. If anything...it intensified as she looked from him to me.

Jeremi, oblivious to her desires, moved without hesitation to take the piece that put him in check. Josselyn pouted, but a sly smile twitched at the corners of her mouth.

"I think if Josselyn wins, we get her the vanity we saw in the city last week for her nameday," I suggested casually.

"Really?" Josselyn's excitement was palpable.

The vanity was an eye-catching piece of ebony with intricate carvings of vines and roses that had captured Josselyn's undivided attention. I was afraid I'd have to lift her over my shoulder and drag her out of the store.

"Perhaps, if you can win..." Jeremi teased her.

Before uttering another breath, Josselyn moved her queen with nothing but confidence. "Checkmate."

"Well, Josselyn, we both heard him say it, did we not?" I kissed Jeremi's cheek as he looked over the board in confusion.

"I...didn't see that." His tone was one of astonishment. "Nice play, sweet."

"Vanity!" she declared, throwing her arms to the sides.

Of course, after such a display. Jeremi couldn't deny her my suggestion. We had the vanity brought in the day of her sixteenth nameday.

IV

osselyn's instincts as a Whisper appeared shortly after reaching adulthood. Despite her traumatic childhood, I would catch her brushing against both Jeremi and me at any chance she could get. And her gaze...the heat never left it.

Prior to Josselyn, I had never looked at a female in terms of companionship. I wasn't closed to the idea—in fact, I was apprehensive to admit to Jeremi that I'd thought of it more than once—but the last thing I wanted was to suggest it to her and destroy all that we'd built upon in three years.

One evening after she'd gone to sleep, I stayed up with Jeremi, sharing a vintage of wine he loved. We were in our bedroom, sitting on cushions we'd thrown about the floor.

"Have you seen it?" I asked, sipping from my glass.

"Hmm?"

"The way she looks at us now."

Jeremi nodded. "With Whispers, their maturing feelings and desires essentially compound much faster than ours do. And that rate doesn't decrease for at least another ten years."

"Now in words I can understand?" I laughed.

"I wouldn't be surprised if she was tearing at our clothing in the next few weeks," he replied calmly, taking a drink.

I blushed, remembering my first time. How Cyprus had been so afraid to hurt me despite me clawing at his tunic. I took another deep sip of wine.

"Will you ever tell her?" Jeremi pondered.

"About what?"

"About Cyprus."

Jeremi was fully supportive of bringing him in as a Ring and understood why it upset me when Cyprus declined. He knew how much I'd loved him; how much I still loved him. "…No, I don't think so."

"Why not?" He seemed legitimately surprised.

"Josselyn is still in such a frail mental state…I just don't…I don't want—" —*to break her,* I thought, but couldn't find the words to explain it. "I want her to feel secure in her home, as the person she is. The less she knows about my previous relations, I think, the better."

"…If that's how you feel, my sweet," he sighed. He didn't agree but he wouldn't press me on it.

"I believe I told her as much as she needed to know, for now. I want her to be able to develop her own feelings for the both of us."

"I understand what you mean, but don't forget your own emotions, love."

"I know, but what do we do about Josselyn's…desires?" I countered.

"We could leave the offer open?" he suggested, polishing off his glass. "I never took you for fancying women."

"I didn't either, really. But I...I'm open to the idea." My words were more sheepish than I'd intended. I wanted to be confident in my statement and I think Jeremi understood that.

His hand found mine and squeezed. "If you do have an interest, I won't be the one to judge you for your feelings. You don't have to hide it from me."

"I wouldn't. Of that, I swear to you." I smiled.

He bent at the waist and kissed me deeply, pushing me to the pillows on the floor.

"I love you," he murmured against my mouth.

"I love you, too." Forever and always.

Jeremi, Josselyn, and I lounged in her room sharing supper and wine. It wasn't often we all dined outside of the dining room, but I wanted so desperately to talk with her away from potentially prying ears. I wanted Josselyn to feel safe in speaking with us, and—not knowing what would occur—let her express herself behind closed doors.

"What's the occasion?" Josselyn giggled as Jeremi poured her another glass. "I didn't miss a nameday, did I?"

"No, my dear, nothing like that." Jeremi smiled.

"We wanted to speak with you about…how you're feeling," I explained carefully.

"I feel fine. I love it here," she replied.

"And that, we're very thankful for." Jeremi touched her hand.

"Josselyn, I suppose, what I mean is…is there anything you yearn for…physically?"

Color raised to her cheeks as her gaze fell to her wine. "I-I…I don't want to speak out of turn…"

"Just say what's on your mind," Jeremi encouraged her.

"I…I think about the both of you…all of the time"

"What do you think about?" I asked, my curiosity peaking.

"About…well, it's not…it's not the most ladylike of ways…to think about two people…" she confessed, taking another sip of her wine. "Was I that obvious?"

"That's not it at all," I insisted quickly. Then chuckled and admitted the truth. "Well, perhaps…a little conspicuous."

"Gods, you must think me a fool." The hue of embarrassment deepened on her face.

"You are no fool, Josselyn. We both wanted to give you an opportunity to…explore that side of yourself," Jeremi explained.

"I-I couldn't possibly! I'd just…I don't want to disappoint you." She drained her glass and swayed a few inches toward Jeremi. The flush of intoxication mingled with her humiliation.

"Of that, you could never do," I assured her. "If there's anything you want right now, then take it."

She glanced at Jeremi, who nodded his concurrence. "…Alright."

Setting her empty glass to the side, she took Jeremi's hand. My heart raced as she crawled to where I was, leading Jeremi behind her. Rearranging her legs so she sat in my lap, she grasped his hands and placed them on her waist. She wrapped her arms around my neck and bent her neck so her forehead touched mine. For a few heart-pounding moments, we lived on each other's breaths.

"Is this…is this alright?" she whispered.

My blood raced and my head spun. She was scared of disappointing us when in truth, I was terrified of disappointing her.

"Yes," I replied under my breath—curious, excited, anxious.

When her lips met mine they were soft and sweet—she tasted of wine and heat. I guided the movement of her mouth and her gentle kisses turned hungry. I was completely taken with her. My fingers wandered across her hips—her body shuddered beneath my touch. Jeremi's hands slowly traced the curves of her torso while his lips caressed her shoulder. I teased her bottom lip with my tongue and her breath caught. She drew away from me.

"Are you alright?" I whispered, worried we'd moved too fast.

"I've never…felt like this…" she moaned when Jeremi's mouth found her ear. "It's…incredible…"

"Let yourself go, love," I urged.

Josselyn turned her head and Jeremi's lips claimed hers. I held her close to me at the waist, kissing her throat, collarbone, above her breast. Her heated skin was silken smooth and her body fought for attentions between my lips and Jeremi's. Every shiver that ran through her only fed my desire. My self-conscious anxieties dispelled, I desperately wanted to explore every unknown inch of her. Even so, I was still terrified to move at a faster pace than Josselyn was comfortable with. So I allowed her to advance as she pleased. She separated from Jeremi, panting.

"I'm...really dizzy," she remarked.

"That could be the wine, my sweet. Or this." He nibbled at her neck and she gasped. He looked at me and smiled—it was devilish and delicious. "Maybe a little of both?"

"Would you like to stop?" I asked. I wanted nothing more than to continue, but her comfort was first.

"I'm scared," she murmured. "I've never craved something so strongly. I can barely think."

I shifted her from my lap to sit between us. I brushed my fingers through her long, brilliant hair and Jeremi took her hand into his.

"Every inch of my body wants to keep going, but I...I'm afraid..."

"It's alright, Josselyn. Really. We'll continue this another night." I thought I hid my feelings well, but a flicker of Jeremi's eyes said he knew perfectly well that was the last thing I wanted.

"Don't ever be afraid to tell us what you want. It's perfectly fine to experience what you're feeling." Jeremi kissed the top of her head.

Whether it was the mutterings of a drunk woman or her truth, we didn't know. She leaned her head against my chest and uttered the words that would bury themselves into my heart for all time.

"I love you, both. Please…let me stay by you always."

V

fter our first encounter together, I feared Josselyn's attitude toward us would change. I couldn't have been more wrong. I found her fingers entwining with mine and Jeremi's when we went into the city. Any space ever left between us she was sure to close, and the way she looked at us—it was no longer just desire, it was the stare of someone who knew what they were missing.

Since Josselyn was officially allowed into taverns, Jeremi suggested we bring her to one we'd heard about in Anastas. The Cursed Elixir, a newer establishment that we'd heard of by word of mouth as being one of the higher quality places for food and drink.

We arrived in the late afternoon and we were greeted by a short-haired, buxom woman carrying a tray of drinks. "One moment, folks and I'll be right there."

The Cursed Elixir was split into two stories—the bottom of which housed the tavern, and an upstairs that I could only assume were its rooms. The lighting was comfortable, tables and floors impeccably clean. Very few patrons were spread out amongst them—I assumed we'd arrived before the dinner rush. The three of us waited patiently at the door for her to serve the mugs and goblets before our greeter came bustling back to us.

"Welcome! I don't think I've seen your faces before," she said cheerfully. She towered over Josselyn and me and fussed at our cloaks like we were children. "I'm Hilde Olrick. My husband Alan and I own the place. We'll be happy to serve you all!"

"Thank you, miss Olrick—" I began.

"No need for that, m'lady. Just Hilde's fine." She carefully lay our cloaks over her large forearm. "Sit anywhere you like. What can I start you off with?"

"A bottle of any red you like, Hilde." Jeremi smiled.

She gave us a little bow and rushed off as we found a booth to sit in. The aromas of cooked meats and freshly baked bread wafted to us as we waited for Hilde to return.

"I like it here," Josselyn stated, taking in her surroundings. "She didn't look at me like...like I'm a demon."

"That's because you aren't, love," I replied.

I saw how many of the citizens still averted their gazes from Josselyn and I understood that there were many I didn't see. I knew it had to have an effect on her and tried my best to allay her concerns. I could only hope that the more time she spent amongst them, the more they'd accept her as their own.

"You're perfect the way you are," Jeremi said, and a grin painted her lips.

"Here we are!" Hilde placed three glasses on the table and poured each one slightly above half, setting the rest of the bottle on the table. "So, let's start with your names, hmm?"

I laughed, accustomed to only being asked for my order. "I'm Victoria, this is my husband, Jeremi, and this is Josselyn."

"Well, Jeremi, whatever your secret is for holding the attention of two beautiful women, cling to it with your life." Hilde winked at him and Josselyn giggled.

"Perhaps I misjudged you, Hilde. Are you asking for assistance in that department?" he replied with a handsome smile. Jeremi was not so easily embarrassed.

Hilde barked a laugh and clapped a hand on his shoulder. "I like you. Next round's on me. What can I get you to eat?"

We each ordered a bowl of the stew that Hilde insisted Alan was known for. She was right, it was delicious. As the night continued, more and more customers filled the tables and the hum of conversation of work days and politics brewed with ours. The three of us enjoyed each other's company…and a lot of wine. I wondered if Jeremi realized we were on our fourth bottle, or if the flush of Josselyn's cheeks aided him in his decision to continue ordering.

"We'd better head home before poor Josselyn can't walk anymore," I remarked while she giggled at one of Jeremi's sly comments.

"Can we come back here? Please?" she pleaded.

"Of course we can. Hilde might drag us all back if we don't," Jeremi replied.

"Good, I'm glad. We can go then." She nodded and as she stood, her body wavered. I was quickly by her side to steady her.

We waved to Hilde and stepped out into the cool evening. Josselyn took our hands and led us toward the estate.

Her skin was hot to the touch.

When we arrived, we guided Josselyn to her chambers. Just outside of the doors, she stopped us.

"What's wrong?" I asked.

"Could I...if it's okay with you both...could I spend the night with you?" she asked sheepishly. I looked to Jeremi and gave him a slight nod.

"We'd love nothing more," he replied and swept Josselyn off of her feet.

She squealed in delight and we both laughed. The wine had slowed my reactions and served to unveil the cravings I'd had since I first felt her lips.

Our room wasn't far from hers—I preferred it that way so we may always be close if she needed anything. Josselyn was already playing at the buttons on Jeremi's tunic as I locked the door behind us. He laid her carefully on the bed and positioned himself beside her. I made my way to her other side and lay against her back.

"If you need to stop, Josselyn, please say so," I advised.

"Mhmm," she hummed her reply, already wrapping my arms around her and pulling Jeremi's mouth against hers.

Josselyn's brilliant hair spilled like a lake on our pillows, her skin a perfect contrast to the satin sheets. Her beauty was picturesque and I so badly wanted to feel her entirely. I traced the outline of her waist, moving to her chest, adjusting my touch to her sounds of pleasure. I kissed her throat and shoulder, enthralled in her taste.

Jeremi's hands moved across Josselyn to me, pulling at the fastenings of my top. My heart raced and I left my attentions to finish what Josselyn had begun with his shirt. Josselyn drew away, realizing our intentions, and helped us both undress before turning unpracticed fingers on her corset. I undid the rest of the ties and she removed it with shaking hands.

She looked at us—all three of us half-naked—and smiled, embarrassed. "I...don't know what to do..."

"Anything you want, sweetheart," I replied.

She turned toward me, pressing her mouth to mine and her hips to Jeremi. Everything I'd done during our first kiss she copied perfectly. It wasn't long until I was gasping for air. Her lips moved to my throat, down to my collar bone, then to tease my breast. I couldn't suppress my moans. I twined my fingers in her hair, his lips claimed mine, his hands found her breasts and her nails dug into my skin.

All of our movements seemed to happen so fast. It was exhilarating.

I pulled Josselyn to meet my mouth and rolled her on her back so Jeremi and I could reciprocate her affections. As the both of us stimulated her skin, her back arched and her breathing quickened. Her fingers wandered the hard lines of Jeremi's back and chest, occasionally caressing my face before searching for new attentions.

"No more...clothes," she gasped, tugging at my skirts.

I laughed beneath my breath and we stripped each other of the rest of our garb. It was the first time the three of us were bared to one other and we took our time drinking in every curve, arch, and line. The sensation of both of their hands on my body was something I could never explain—it set my heart alight and my skin ablaze. Josselyn's motions fit in perfectly with ours. Her body was like a missing piece to a puzzle we never realized needed solving. She took Jeremi's hand and moved it to her thigh.

"Are you sure?" he murmured against her hair.

"Yes," she sighed.

Heartbeats after Jeremi slid his fingers inside of her, her entire body clenched. She plunged her tongue down my throat and groaned in ecstasy.

"Well, that didn't take long." Jeremi chuckled.

She leaned her forehead against mine, freeing herself to speak.

"I-I'm sorry." She blushed furiously.

"It's alright." I smiled. Her senses were overloaded, her reaction was expected. "Would you like to stop?"

"No, not yet." She lifted her gaze, and her eyes burned for more. "Please."

I can't say to what hour the three of us stayed awake memorizing each point of the other's pleasure. When we finally collapsed from exhaustion, I could see the sun peeking through the windows. Josselyn lay between us and we held her close. Jeremi's fingers intertwined with mine. It was the first soundless sleep I'd experienced in a long time.

VI

The dynamic between Jeremi and I drastically changed upon the addition of Josselyn to our relationship. I found myself even more protective of her when we went into the city. Jeremi would take a day off of work at even the slightest sign of her discomfort. She shared in our joys and sadness, in our outings and in our bed. We'd developed from a husband and wife to a husband, wife, and their lover. And…that's exactly what she was. We loved her. After ten years of our continued courtship, I took Jeremi aside for one of the most difficult conversations I'd ever shared with him.

"What's on your mind, love?" he asked.

We were seated beneath the pavilion that Jeremi held his reading and writing sessions with Josselyn. I cradled a cup of tea that I'd nursed since we sat down, despite the full teapot that sat waiting in the middle of the table.

"I want…I want to ask Josselyn to be our Ring," I admitted. There wasn't any reason to dance around it.

Jeremi carefully set his glass of water on the table. "Victoria, we frequent the same places. So I'm sure you've heard about—"

"That Whispers are vanishing? That the Church of Elwyn has declared that being a Ring is no better than being a prostitute?" I sighed. "You and I would never let harm come to Josselyn. If that means we keep a closer eye on her, then I believe we have that power."

"I don't want to put her even *more* at risk of a zealot striking her down." Jeremi ran a hand through his hair and sighed. "However, that's not to say I haven't thought the same thing."

"Why didn't you say anything?" I was surprised. We were always so open with what we were thinking.

"Honestly, sweet, with how upset you were when Cyprus declined...I never wanted to subject you to that again."

I understood what he meant. Even though it was so many years prior, Cyprus' decline had dealt me an incredible blow. I'd tried to hide it when I received the rejection, but I was inconsolable for days.

"I'll understand if she doesn't want to. However, I think it's only fair to give her the option. I know what she means to you and what she means to me. If there's a way for her to solidify the three of us together...well, wouldn't you want that, too?" I asked.

"I don't disagree with you, at all. If it's what she wants, then I'll be happy to oblige."

"I'm glad." I took a sip of my water. "Jeremi, there's...one other thing I want to talk to you about."

"Anything."

"I know what you said about Adrien. About what he's done in terms of making your family business even more depraved. There must be a way to stop him. There has to be someone higher we can go to."

"I told you, I've wanted nothing more. But, his web of corruption extends further than I'm familiar with. I don't know if it's a possibility."

"There has to be something. Paperwork, the contract we have, anything he's said in writing to you. We could encourage him to take it down from the inside with evidence."

"You want to blackmail him?"

"I'm sorry…I'm not familiar with that word," I confessed.

"It's exactly what you explained. Threatening him with evidence so he closes the business down himself," he explained calmly. "Adrien's not a monster, but I don't know the rest of his colleagues."

"Jeremi, think about what an amazing impact Josselyn has had on our relationship. Even if it's not the same kind, what if any of those people auctioned could give someone else even half of that happiness? I'm sure they have dreams and wishes, too. Then nothing ever comes of them—because they were sold for coin."

"…You make it impossible to say 'no.' I hope you know that," he resigned. "I'll talk to him."

"Thank you so much, love. You've no idea what this means to me." I embraced him and he kissed my hair.

"Start thinking of what you'd like to say to Josselyn."

VII

Dear Cyprus,

I hope this finds you well. I know a fair amount of time has passed since my last letter. Jeremi and I asked Josselyn to be our Ring and she accepted. We had to wait for this season's illness to pass in order to visit the Temple that performs the ceremony. I hope you managed to evade becoming ill—Josselyn wasn't so lucky and was stuck in bed for a fortnight. Thankfully, she's doing much better. Just healing from her tattoo.

The three of us visited the Cursed Elixir again last night. You would absolutely adore Hilde. She's funny, kind, and has one of the best selections of wine in the city. The patrons don't seem to drink to excess—in truth, I think they're afraid of what Hilde would do to them if they were too rowdy.

I was in Lorelyn a few months ago. Gwen told me she forwards my letters to you at your new residence. She was vague on the circumstances, but whatever they are, I pray you're happy. You deserve everything you want in this life. My parents were, well, predictable. Mother asked how you were doing. Father focused on my new life in Anastas. It was wonderful to see them. I just hope one day they have the chance to visit outside of the Istens. As I hope for you.

This spring, the flowers in my gardens are doing beautifully. With Josselyn's help, we were able to weave the ivy up the walls of the estate and plant even more flowers. Their nectar seemed to attract an interesting type of butterfly that I've never seen before. Beautiful purple wings nearly the size of my hand. I must confess, I've spent more time than I care to admit on trying to attract one onto my hand. Josselyn succeeds without a second thought. Perhaps they can still sense the snow that once frequented my skin.

I miss you, Cyprus. I hope one day you'll make the journey down to Anastas to visit and see it for yourself. I wish so badly to introduce you to Josselyn. Jeremi and I would love to host you in our home.

Please take care of yourself and I look forward to your response.

Tere L'etai, my sweet.

Love Always,

Victoria

REACT

BOOK THREE
OF
WHISPERS FROM THE PAST

I

I held a cool cloth to my blackened eye. Bruises and scrapes decorated my pale arms and legs. Thankfully I wasn't bleeding too much—and most of it wasn't mine. The other kid would miss a few days of tutelage.

"Where is she?" I heard my father's booming voice from down the hall. I hadn't expected him to be happy, but his tone was unnerving.

I sucked on a split knuckle in an attempt to ease the sting. When he rounded the corner, he assessed the situation and shook his head.

"Come on, Isabelle," he commanded.

I stood without hesitation.

"You have to admit, sir, she has your fire," the man watching over me commented.

"Aye, too much for a girl. Let's go." With that, he turned heel and I trailed behind him.

I concentrated on the ground as he led me outside of my language tutor's estate. His strides were long and sure. I had to skip steps to keep up with him.

"Why this time?" he asked with the authority I usually associated with his work.

"Stephan said I was just a stupid girl. When I told him to shut up he called me a bitch," I explained under my breath.

"Surely, beating him to submission proved him wrong." Father glowered down at me from the corner of his eye.

"Lord Radcliff says that's the worst thing you can call a lady!" I retorted.

"I would agree with Lord Radcliff. However, my daughter is no lady."

I felt tears of anger well up in my eyes. I hid them with the cloth.

"Do you prefer to be called 'Sir Garrett Rhodes' brat?'"

"No!"

"I've heard it from your instructors, Isabelle. You are ten years old now and if a boy calls you a name you ignore him. If you so badly want to be a lady, then act like it."

My empty fingers balled into a fist but I couldn't maintain it very long—pain seared across my knuckles. My joints ached and the cuts burned. I said nothing and held back my complaints.

In Father's eyes, I should have been on the worse end of the fight.

When we arrived home, my mother took one look at me and rushed me into the washroom, ordering a servant to fetch hot water. She carefully moved my hand that held the towel and looked at my black eye.

"Oh sweet, haven't you learned?" she admonished.

"I couldn't help it...Stephan called me awful names..." I touched the cloth back to my throbbing cyc.

"Get yourself out of those filthy clothes. I'll be right back." She kissed my forehead and returned to the front room.

I didn't have the chance to undress before the bickering drifted through the door.

"Elaine, how else am I supposed to teach her what she's doing is wrong?" Father bellowed.

"Not by ignoring her!"

"You remember the last time she boxed a peer? This is nothing compared to that!"

I sighed as I slipped off my skirts. He wasn't wrong—Lady Millie had threatened to never teach me again if I ever lay a hand on another one of her students. But Patrick had said the most vile things about my mother...

"Garrett, you need to be her father, not her bailiff," Mother said as the servant filled the tub to completion.

I carefully stepped into the near-scalding water. Air hissed through my teeth when every open cut was exposed to the bath and it took me longer than usual to settle myself. Mother returned just as I settled, the water sitting comfortably at my neckline.

"I'm sorry, Is. Let's get you cleaned up."

Unfortunately, it wasn't the last fight I'd find myself in.

II

My lessons continued and over the next few years, I learned to better control my sensitive temperament. Though, beating the fear of the gods into a few of the boys may have helped with that.

Father thought it appropriate to start me in the ways of music, painting, and etiquette at the age of thirteen. I bit my tongue and suffered through them, bored out of my mind. The other girls—listening with rapt attention—followed the instructors perfectly while I struggled with the concepts of 'art' and wondered why it was important to place one's spoon to the right of their knife. As time passed, I fell in love with an unexpected subject. One I realized by accident.

My home city of Maura was a quiet one—only the basic necessities filled our city square. Veritas, the city to the southwest, was a major trading post due to its position between Valford and the Capital. Maura was out of the way—stranded to east—and held only the promise of high-quality iron. Even so, our quarries were taken up by the citizens of the city and outsiders were violently chased away, forced to pay their weight in gold for the material. The tranquility due to the lack of visitors held a surprising opportunity—the ability for me to enjoy the evening sky atop a hill a fair distance from my home.

Nearly every night after supper, I would excuse myself and—much to my father's displeasure—take my horse to that hill. More than a handful of times I was positive he sent a servant to follow me. But, when he found that his daughter did nothing but lie in the grass and stare into the heavens, I'm sure he thought me mad and called the servant off.

In truth, the stars fascinated me. These mysterious beings of light that stories and legends associated with souls and wishes. Each one seemed to have its own specific place in the sky. Eventually, I brought a journal with me and under the light of a dim lantern attempted to map the locations of the brightest ones, making up names for them as I went along.

I knew my father wanted nothing more than to tell me I was wasting my time, filling my silly head with ideas. But the project kept me out of trouble during my studies and my instructors had nothing but good things to say about my performance. My mother secretly packed me snacks to eat, attaching the satchel to my horse in the afternoons. It was her own small rebellion against my father and I loved her more for it.

After one of my many language lessons with Lord Radcliff, I was collecting my pens and papers when he took a seat next to me at the table.

"Isabelle, may I see that?" He motioned to my journal, in which I'd painstakingly tracked many nights of the evening sky.

"It…has nothing to do with learning language, my lord," I replied. I couldn't keep the edge from my tone—my work was extremely personal to me. I didn't need another reason for my father to tell me to get my head out of the clouds and a word from my instructor would do just that.

"I know," he chuckled. "I'm not going to keep it, I saw you looking through it earlier and I was curious."

I eyed him carefully and slid the book his way. He opened it and turned the pages as if he were unfolding the petals on a flower. Nodding as he thumbed through my hundreds of notes and dozens of charts, he closed the cover and handed it back to me.

"When did you become interested in astronomy?" he asked.

"I didn't realize stargazing had another name."

"This isn't just stargazing you're working on, my dear. If the stars are just to gaze at, then why chart them?"

I felt embarrassed. I wasn't sure how to explain myself. "You'll think it's stupid," I murmured.

"That's for me to decide, isn't it?" He smiled. I felt a little better. He was one of the few adults in my life who had my respect and understood my wild temper.

"I just…I realized that sometimes they move. I try to track the brightest ones and over time, when I'd go to mark them down, they're in a new spot," I admitted.

I opened my journal and pointed to three different stars I'd found easiest to record. I'd named them Elwyn, Naya, and Brynn after the three goddesses of legend. "Like these ones. Eventually, they come back to the same place. But they definitely move."

"That's not stupid at all. You're very intelligent, Isabelle. Aptly named stars, too." He nodded and I blushed. "Let me show you something." He stood and walked to a closed off room in the back of his home.

I followed without a word, curiosity piqued my interest.

"This is my study," he announced upon my entry. "I don't often invite people back here. However, I believe you could benefit."

The first thing to catch my eye was a huge, hand-drawn parchment that nearly covered an entire wall. There were circles within circles, lines leading from the center outward and dotting its entirety—little stars with names painstakingly written next to them. Some were connected and had faint drawings of what the shape made—animals, ships, people. I stared at it in awe, tracing my fingertips over the clusters I recognized.

"Why a circle to represent the sky?" I asked, thinking within the rectangular confines of my journal.

Lord Radcliff plucked a small, golden instrument from his desk and handed it to me. It was thick and flat, containing multiple circles similar to his giant sky map and dozens of etchings of lines and tiny numbers.

"What is this?" I turned it over in my hands, the smooth metal cool against my fingers.

"It's called an astrolabe."

"How does this answer my question about your map?"

"Well, the world we live upon is round, like this circle here," he explained, outlining the center sphere. "It rotates so slowly that you and I can't feel it. But when it does—" He knelt next to me and pushed one of the pieces on the edge so it moved smoothly around the surface. "—The sky, or the part that's shifting now, will change position."

I didn't realize I'd stopped breathing. I was enthralled by the idea that I was a small piece of something so much larger. That outside the door of my estate was more than hills and mountains and trees, but this expanse of ever-changing sky.

"Lord Radcliff...how can I learn more about the stars?" I asked, experimenting with different pieces of the astrolabe.

"There's a university in Ordehl—"

"The Kingdom next to us?" It seemed so far away. Though, in truth, the border was closer to Maura than we were to Valford.

"Mhmm. A day's ride from the border is a city named Myrin and within it a far better university than any in Rhoryn. I may be biased, however, as I did teach there." He smirked and stood.

"Why did you leave?"

"Teaching hundreds of students a year eventually wore me down. I retired to Maura where it's much quieter and I only have a few of you at a time." He moved to a tall bookcase, leaving me to study the astrolabe once more. "Unfortunately, astronomy isn't needed as much in a small city like this one. So I changed my focus to teaching language."

"I'm sorry if I've been a terrible student," I murmured, knowing that most of my fights started within his lessons.

He laughed. "Not at all, little one. I believe you and I both know Stephan Vigroux is a detestable twat." He pulled a tome from one shelf and paused mid-movement. "That is between you and me, understand?"

"Of course, m'lord." I giggled and he handed me the book. It was heavy and I had to place the astrolabe back on his desk to thumb through it.

Hundreds of pages on stars, the world's movements, and the history of astronomy. All carefully penned and bound in leather.

"You won't be able to enter the university until you're sixteen. However, I don't see why you and I can't get a head start on your studies." He gestured casually, but he could see right through me.

I would love nothing more. "Truly?"

"After your regular lessons with me, bring that book with you, and we'll go through it chapter by chapter. If we finish it, I have more. We can study for as long as you like."

"Thank you, my lord," I replied, breathless with excitement.

"Take care of my book as if it were your own, understand?"

"Of course, sir. Do I look like a detestable twat to you?"

III

Lord Radcliff was well versed in astronomy and I was an attentive student. We began with mathematics— something I didn't associate with the night sky. I found it to be the most difficult part of my studies. Even so, he was just as patient as always and I kept at it with fervor. When he found my understanding adequate, we moved on to charts, star names, how they moved and why. Every lesson was something new and I devoured it.

Shortly after my fifteenth nameday, I returned home from my instruction one evening to find my father in the sitting room with another man. Father was more relaxed than I'd seen him in months and they laughed with ease. All I could see of his guest was his dark hair as he faced my father.

"I'm home," I announced, dutifully slipping off my shoes in the doorway.

"Ah, Isabelle, I have someone I'd like you to meet," my father replied.

I couldn't remember the last time he'd smiled at me. I approached the sitting room as they both stood. My heart skipped as I met the steady, silver gaze of his guest. I wanted to hide behind the book in my arms.

"This is Adrien Markov. He's a luxury goods tradesman from Valford. Adrien, this is my daughter, Isabelle." It was the kindest I'd ever heard my father say my name.

"A pleasure." I curtsied, my heart racing.

Adrien was young—he couldn't have been thirty yet. Errant strands of his dark hair fell across his eyes. He was all hard lines and soft edges—he was strikingly handsome.

He took my hand into his own and brushed his lips across my knuckles. "The pleasure's mine, I assure you."

I could feel the color rise from my neck to my cheeks and I looked to the floor in embarrassment.

"Be mindful, Adrien. This kitten has claws." My father chuckled.

"Father," I rebuked.

"I see no kitten here." Adrien shifted the hair covering my face behind my ear. "A rose, perhaps."

I met his unwavering gaze. I was no delicate flower to be picked. "Thorns it is, then," I replied. To my surprise, he laughed. The melodic sound stroked my skin in an unfamiliar way and I shivered.

"I like your spirit, Isabelle," Adrien remarked. He turned to my father. "Forgive me, Master Rhodes, but I really must go. I'm glad we could come to an agreement."

"As am I, Adrien." Father clasped hands with him and pat him on the shoulder like an old friend. "Find your way home safely and we'll be in touch."

Adrien faced me once more and bowed. That's when I saw it— flames infinitely burning behind silver. For a brief moment, I wanted to melt in them. "I hope to see you again, my lady."

"Likewise," I replied, fighting to keep composure.

Adrien took his leave and I took a seat in the chair Adrien had occupied just moments before. The cushions were still warm.

"He seems...nice." I struggled to find a word to describe him.

"Looks like he took a shining to you." He chuckled and poured himself another glass of brandy. "Very powerful businessman, that one."

I rolled my eyes. "I'm not one for pet names."

"I've heard Valford is quite beautiful. He mentioned needing a few good people to help around his estate."

"I doubt he had me in mind." I bit my lip, wondering if I should take the plunge and have the discussion I'd waited two years for. I couldn't remember the last time I'd seen my father in such high spirits and knew there would be no better opportunity.

I took a deep breath, pushing the image Adrien's intense gaze out of my mind. "Father, may we talk?"

"What is it?" The red tinges of intoxication colored his face.

"In a year I'll be sixteen—"

"An adult! About time." He laughed.

"Yes...and I'd...I'd like to go to Myrin. To the university."

His demeanor shifted completely—it was alarming. He was back to Bailiff Rhodes, the man who must always keep me in line. "What for?"

I hugged the book I'd come to love so much given to me by Lord Radcliff. "To study astronomy."

"What use is that to a girl?"

I felt the first flickers of anger. "What use is it to anyone? I don't find knowledge of how our world works useless, Father. And Lord Radcliff said he would write me a letter of recommendation—"

"So he's been putting all these silly ideas into your head?"

"Father, I have never asked anything of you. I want this...more than anything."

"You expect me to pay your entry into this place?"

"If I have to wait tables at the tavern, I will. If all you want to give me is your blessing, so be it. If I don't have that, well, I certainly won't be surprised."

"Isabelle—"

"All I've ever wanted was to make you proud. To not tarnish our name. Your reputation earned me no friends, granted me no quarter, and you want me to stand by and keep my mouth shut. If you don't wish to support this either, fine." I stood, holding back the tears that threatened to give me away. I was consumed in frustration and fury.

"Isabelle, you don't—" His voice rose to a yell and I wasn't going to hear it.

"Yes, I do." I turned heel and left him sitting alone, making my way past my curious mother to my room.

I should have anticipated our talk to go exactly as it had. But the tears that soaked my pillow told me I'd expected otherwise.

Father made no more mention of my going to the university after it was clear I'd made up my mind. I spent the year working side jobs to anyone who would hire me, stashing away every last coin I made. My studies continued, but I neglected the etiquette courses in favor of more time learning with Lord Radcliffe. My moments at home were reserved for sleeping and that was all—my days started early and ended late.

My mother supported me in quiet ways: packing snacks for me, leaving me a few extra coins for supplies and food stalls. On one occasion, I found a stunning necklace in my room with a small star pendant. I wore it as a reminder of what I was working so hard to accomplish.

A few months after I turned sixteen, I counted my savings and resolved that I had enough for both the entrance fees and to keep myself afloat until I could find work in Myrin. I packed all of my sensible clothing, my book, money, and my necklace. I left behind the great gowns I was forced to wear to gatherings—there would be no need for them at the university. My things were perfectly folded and arranged to fit on my horse, which I'd also informed Mother I would be taking.

The morning of my departure, I entered the main hall of our estate and Father was there waiting for me. His posture was that of a guard waiting to take the guilty into custody.

I squared my shoulders and walked passed him.

"Isabelle—" My name was used as a command.

I paused and waited in silence.

"You're making a mistake," he stated.

"A mistake?" I laughed dryly. "A year to think of this conversation and all you have to say is that I'm making a mistake?"

"You could marry a noble, live a happier life. This…ambition of yours—it's unrealistic."

I turned to face him. Unrealistic. As if he knew. "Goodbye, Father."

"Adrien has been asking about you."

I paused, remembering Adrien's lips on my hand, his dark hair, the fire in his eyes…

"Let him keep asking." I closed the gap between me and the door. "Perhaps he'll find someone more…qualified."

And with that, I made my way to Myrin.

IV

yrin was like nothing I'd ever seen. A handful of miles outside of the city, the barren landscape turned to sand—a desert. Ordehl was beautiful in its own right but very different from the green, lush environments of Rhoryn. The city of Myrin was made up of its university, housing, as well as a strip of shops and traders. It was only a touch busier than Maura at its peaks, but the people spoke many different languages and the culture was rich.

Fortunately, with previous letters I'd sent to the head of the university, along with Lord Radcliff's letter of recommendation and my entrance fee, becoming a student was easier than I'd expected. I rented a small room right on the outskirts of the school and found work almost immediately in the only tavern in Myrin.

Classes were difficult and rigorous—I spent many evenings both working and studying for exams. I was one of three women in the program and drew a lot of unwanted attention from my peers, but did my best to ignore it. A few of them took to teasing me when they discovered I waited tables after classes. Afraid of expulsion, I let them have their fun and was thankful when they gave up when it didn't bring a rise out of me.

A few months in, a package arrived. It was penned in Lord Radcliff's steady hand and inside it contained a letter of encouragement, a bag of coins for use as I saw fit, and the small astrolabe I had played with so long before. The thoughtful gift moved me to tears as I hadn't heard so much as a word from my parents. I replied post haste.

I grew accustomed to the desert air and climate. I learned that the landscape was perfect for viewing the sky at night—there were rarely any clouds and very little obtrusive lighting in the city. I learned to use telescopes, to read star charts more efficiently, and to operate different tools that used the stars to tell time and distance. By the end of the first year, if I ever found myself on a ship lost at sea, I could lead them home. The opportunities and studies seemed endless and I soaked in every drop.

My second year was filled with more in-depth mathematics that had to do with the world's movements and positioning in relation to the sky. These subjects I knew to be my weakest. I tackled them with a hunger known only by the recklessly determined. I continued my work at the tavern despite my studies increasing and slept little. During one of my shifts, a handsome young man from my class stopped by for a drink.

"Isabelle, take the night off and have a drink with me." He toasted me after I served him his ale.

The owner of the tavern, a nosy little gremlin of a woman with a temper like mine, watched the entire exchange. Despite her drawbacks, I was the hardest worker she had and she insisted I do what my classmate suggested.

"How are you, Owen?" I slipped into the booth with him, holding a mug of my own ale.

"Better, now that I've discovered where you spend your nights." He smiled, hazel eyes sparkling.

"How long have you searched?" I laughed. I was surprised that anyone would want to find me.

"Ages, my lady! Far and wide. And lo, here you are!" Owen gestured grandly with his arms, strands of his chestnut hair flailed wildly. He had a flair for the dramatic.

"How disappointed you must be to discover your prize is a tavern wench," I said, rolling my eyes.

"Not at all! It's charming, really. The top of our class serves drinks to the bottom feeders. Poetic."

"Mhmm, pure poetry." I took a hefty swig of my drink and we ordered something to eat.

We shared polite conversation about classes and instructors, nibbling on our food. Owen was the first person in Myrin to approach me as a friend and not just a girl who could offer both ale and test answers. It was the most comfortable I'd felt in my entire time living there.

"How do you manage to ward off all the other men, Isabelle?"

"What other men?" I laughed. "I feel I intimidate most of them, really."

"Well! Then you must allow me to treat you this evening," Owen replied, abashed.

"Owen, no, you don't have to—"

"No, my Lady, I insist!"

And so, energized by the courage of alcohol and the thrill of the evening, I let Owen take me to bed. I didn't know what to expect. Of course, I knew what it meant to make love to someone, but all of the subtleties? That was a completely different subject. He was gentle and kind, we were awkward and sensual. I couldn't have asked for a better first partner.

Owen and I remained best friends and lovers for the remainder of the year. We studied together—often times in nothing but our underthings—stargazed together, and spent many nights in the comfort of each other's arms. I remained at the top of my class and dragged Owen up with me—even if he whined and complained most of the way.

In the middle of our third year, he was called home to Ashai, which lay more than a week's ride from Myrin. His family desperately needed him to help support them through that years' illness, forcing him to drop out of his studies. He promised to write and for a while, he did. I was heartbroken, but when the letters eventually stopped I understood that the distance was too much.

At the beginning of my fourth year, my exhaustion began to take its toll. I found myself more sluggish in my studies and my work. The owner noticed and insisted I take a few days' rest, offering to cover my wages despite not being there. I gratefully accepted her offer on the few consecutive days I didn't have classes. I slept and relaxed, studied intermittently, and took walks through Myrin in the cool evenings.

On my last night off from work and instruction, I took a longer walk than usual. I stared up at the clear, beautiful night sky, naming the constellations, the stars, recognizing them like old acquaintances. They sparkled their greetings back to me and I smiled—having the knowledge of their system was empowering to me. I made my way back to my small residence and opened the door.

I noticed his shadow far too late.

I was shoved without remorse to the floor of my room. I landed on my hands and knees, rolling to my back in time to see my door closed and a form dive on top of me. I kicked my legs furiously, swung my arms in a desperate attempt to throw my attacker off of me. He shifted his body so the brunt of his weight was on my legs, one of his arms pinning my wrists to the floor above my head. I screamed profanities until I saw the glint of steel in the moonlight.

"If you don't want to be cut to ribbons, I suggest you stay quiet." His voice was low, smooth, hungry.

I swallowed hard, searching for my own voice. "Who the hell are you?"

"I'm disappointed you don't remember, Isabelle," he replied.

My eyes finally adjusted and my breath caught. His hair was shocking white, skin tanned, blue eyes near aglow in the darkness. I'd seen him around between classes—the only Whisper in the school. His race, however, wasn't what separated him from the other students.

Sylus' father owned the university.

"Sylus, what are you doing?" I murmured. I couldn't recall if we'd ever exchanged words.

"Taking what I want. You're a difficult woman to find." He sheathed the knife at his hip and his lips caressed my throat. "You smell amazing."

"Couldn't just ask?"

"That's not nearly as exciting." The smile twisting his lips made my heart leap to my throat.

"You're a bastard," I hissed.

Rage flowed through my veins, overtaking my fear. I yanked one hand free from beneath his arm and before he could react, snatched the dagger from its sheath. I drew it up and underneath his arm, cleanly slicing through his bicep. Blood stained his tunic, pooling on the floor and soaking through my clothes.

"You little bitch!" He tore the knife from my hand and threw it across the room. It skid along the floor until it struck the wall with a *clang*.

I fought against his grip with every fiber of my being, almost able to push him off of me due to his new injury. He grabbed my shoulders and thrust me against the stone floor, the back of my head connecting with the solid ground. White bursts clouded my eyes and a black haze surrounded my vision. He flipped me onto my stomach and tore at my skirts. I kicked at him again, sending a violent shock to my skull. I closed my eyes, dizzy from the pain.

"Your father…will have your head for this." I clawed at the floor with sluggish fingers and…he laughed.

"He'll have *you* hanged if he believes you're lying."

"I'm the best student he has!" Blood gathered beneath my fingernails from my efforts to crawl away.

"Ah yes, but you work at the tavern."

"That has nothing to do with this—"

"You haven't heard the rumors that you'll turn tricks for money?" He cleared my skirts away and tangled a hand into my hair.

"…You're lying." I felt sick.

"So you see, when you asked me for a go, I politely declined. Then you ran to my father with false accusations."

"Please, don't…" Rage gave way to anxiety.

"I think the odds are against you, love." His voice was at my ear.

"Sylus, please—" I didn't understand what I'd done to draw his attention. The sinking sensation in my stomach sealed the terrifying realization that I'd done nothing wrong. This was a game to him.

He pulled hard on my hair, fingers wrapped in the chain of my star necklace. I felt the chain snap and I whimpered.

"Beg more, sweet," he purred.

Damn him. Like hell I would give him everything he wanted. I remained silent.

Sylus did everything he desired to me and I could do nothing. I was powerless to fight back.

I hated him. I hated him more than I'd ever hated anything in my entire life.

When he was finally spent, he tossed me aside like a doll and found his dagger.

"If you want to tell my father, feel free. But if he doesn't kill you, I will," he threatened. "Which would be a damn shame."

I glowered at him in silence.

He looked me over one last time and took his leave.

I dragged my knees to my chest and allowed the sobs I'd withheld for hours to consume me. He'd violated me under the cover of night. My evening sky had betrayed me.

I hated Myrin. I hated Sylus. I hated Whispers.

Hours passed and I struggled to move. It took every last ounce of will I had to change, gather my things and pack my horse. I glanced at my star pendant, hearing it snap all over again. I left it and began my travels when the sun had barely peeked over the horizon.

I journeyed to Valford in four blurred days with a map and my knowledge of the sky to guide me. I couldn't keep food down and drank very little. I was in an immense amount of pain but continued to press on until I was numb to it. Sleep never came. Every time I closed my eyes, I could see Sylus' face; feel his hands and his body against me. I rode on through the remaining evenings, carried only by the sheer determination to escape Myrin.

Finding the estate was simple—everyone in the city revered him like a god. When a servant called him into the main hall to meet me, his look of bewilderment changed quickly to concern.

"Adrien...I didn't know where else to go..." I murmured, paying particular attention to the spinning ground.

"Isabelle, are you alright? You look like you've seen a ghost," he said gently, taking a step toward me.

"No, I…I need help…"

I was tired, miserable, used. I don't remember fainting.

V

hen consciousness returned, I lay in a bed beneath soft sheets and dressed in a fresh nightgown. Adrien sat in a chair beside me, thumbing through a book. When he noticed me awake, he set it down and turned his attentions my direction.

"I had the girls clean you up and dress you. I hope that's alright," he explained.

I nodded. I felt empty and betrayed. Four years of my life vanished in a single night. I heard my father's last warning. *You're making a mistake.*

"Isabelle, do you want to tell me what happened?" Adrien's hand moved to my cheek where he brushed away a stray tear.

Despite his soft touch and kind eyes, I flinched away. I didn't want to be caressed or touched. I wanted to scrub at my skin until it felt clean again. I wanted the sensations of Sylus' body to stop haunting me.

"It's alright if you don't." Adrien studied me, his face painted in worry.

"I'm sorry." I sighed, touching my cheek. He deserved to know why I showed up on his doorstep. "Just be patient with me, please."

I carefully recounted to him my story from the night Adrien first appeared in my home. My father's attitude, my decision to go to the university, even Father's claim of my decision being a mistake. I recounted my classes, my triumphs, my failures. And then I told him about Sylus.

"Isabelle…I'm so sorry." Adrien held his hand open to me and I took it. "Did you tell anyone?"

"No, I was terrified. I couldn't go back to my father and admit that he was right. That all of this was a mistake."

"I don't think it was a mistake at all." He brushed his thumb across my knuckles. "Do not let one bastard destroy your life."

I managed a wry smile. "Well, that 'one bastard' did just send me packing from the life I always wanted. And now…Now I don't know what to do."

"I could use an assistant around here. Someone who knows bookkeeping, math, perhaps a little literature. Would you happen to know anyone like that?" He flashed a disarming smile—his charm was contagious.

"Math and literature, most definitely. Bookkeeping may take a little training."

"Well, the training I can give. As well as room and board. Perhaps also an offer of a night spent in the city every so often?"

"Adrien, you don't have to—"

"You came to me for help, and I'm here to offer it, my lady," he interjected. "So let me help?"

"…Alright." I nodded.

Adrien squeezed my hand and took his book from the nightstand. "Rest for now. When you're feeling better, we'll speak again."

Adjusting to life in Adrien's estate was easier than I'd expected. He commanded his servants show me respect equal to his status and the girls were decent enough. One young woman, in particular, seemed to need my constant supervision. Lily, barely thirteen and learning to work in the kitchens, had gained employment from Adrien through her mother—a longstanding acquaintance of his. She wasn't stupid—by all means, she had the aptitude to do anything she wanted. However, nothing I ever told her seemed to stick. Most of the meals she cooked may have stood up and walked away if I hadn't taken over.

Adrien was a gracious host, providing me with all he promised and more. My own chambers, wardrobe, stimulating conversation, and more money than I'd ever earned while working multiple jobs. Despite my family's prominent name and status, they never offered me the luxuries that Adrien gifted so freely. Expensive perfumes, unexpected presents of jewelry—anything I ever made mention of was given to me without a request for compensation.

For bookkeeping, the work he required was simple enough: mostly the copying of serial numbers, totals, and record keeping. As my father had said, Adrien dealt in auctioning luxury goods that required careful attention and documentation. The slips I copied from contained names, signatures, and the item number. However, there wasn't an explanation of the items sold. I found myself curious, but not enough to put my only sanctuary at risk.

I often thought of the university and my studies. I caught myself more often than not out on the balcony of my room staring up at the sky. Realizing just how far certain stars were out of reach. Not unlike my dreams. Even those remained nightmares.

Too many nights I woke up in a panicked sweat after once again seeing Sylus' cold blue eyes bore into me, feeling his body weigh me to the floor, the metallic scent of his blood on my clothing. I knew I was somewhere he could never find me again. Even so, it was a fear that won out against logic.

Time moved on without my notice and I eased into the weave of daily life as Adrien's assistant. In the evenings I would read, devouring every piece of literature in the estate. It didn't matter the topic or author—my passion for learning had crept its way inside of my heart once more. Over supper, I enjoyed speaking with Adrien about the books I adored and the ones I didn't, and he was a rapt listener. On more than one occasion, I found a new book sitting on my vanity—the subject matter related to the previous night's discussion.

Months passed and the rift in my heart slowly stitched itself back together. The nightmares dissipated and the gaping emotional wounds Sylus inflicted on me healed to scars.

One evening after I'd finished making sure the servants completed all of their tasks, Adrien approached me.

"Isabelle, come to dinner with me?" His smile set my heart racing.

"But, m'lord, don't we always have dinner together?" I smirked.

"No, little rose, clean yourself up and we'll go into the city."

Normally when I went into Valford, it was to pick up newly tailored clothing from Edmund, a book or two from Martin, or ingredients we were missing in the kitchen. Never had I gone into the city for elegant luxuries. I dressed in a gown Adrien had purchased for me weeks prior and took the time to bring out my eyes and lips with cosmetics I'd barely touched since arriving at the estate.

When I found Adrien waiting for me in the main hall, he drank me in from head to toe. I looked to the floor and he closed the space between us with a few easy strides. His hand tipped my chin upward to meet his gaze.

"Why do you hide your face?" he murmured.

"The way you look at me..." I forced my eyes to his. The flames I'd seen so long ago still flickered behind molten silver. "I don't know what to think of it."

His fingers moved from my chin to my cheek, caressing the skin below my ear, his thumb following the structure of my face. A shiver I couldn't suppress slid down my spine. He leaned his forehead to mine and my heart raced. He was so close I could feel the heat from his body.

"How do you *feel,* then?" he whispered, his lips a breath away from my own.

"...Dizzy..." I replied, air evading me.

His mouth claimed mine, erasing logic and thought. When his tongue teased my lips I offered him no resistance. Adrien's gentle embrace, the curious explorations of his tongue—every one of his movements was a question, an askance—*is this alright?*

I wanted him, burned for him as he did for me. The careful quandaries of his motions made me want to force my will upon his. Of course it was alright, it was more than alright. For years I'd wondered what it would be like to be consumed by his fire, and now...Now it was mine.

I wrapped my arms around his waist and pulled him closer to me, erasing all distance between us. The soft strokes of his tongue I responded to with passionate demands of my own. When I elicited his moans my heart skipped a beat.

"Should…we skip dinner?" His words were warm against my lips.

"Skip?" I laughed beneath my breath. "I believe my dinner's right here."

I pushed him backward into the dining hall and closed the great doors behind me.

"Fitting." He smirked and I silenced him with my mouth. "I guess you *are* hungry."

"You have no idea," I whispered, yanking his silk tunic over his head.

In mere heartbeats, we were naked to each other, and every inch of my flesh that came into contact with his was set ablaze. His fingertips grazed my skin while mine searched his with a fervor I hadn't experienced since I'd been with Owen. He pulled me toward the table and lay back on the smooth surface. I crawled on top of him, my knees gliding against the mahogany, his hands tracing the lines of my stomach as I aligned my body to his.

"I love you, Isabelle," Adrien whispered against my lips.

My breath caught at his words. I searched for my reply and found it easier to say than I expected. "I…I love you too."

He smiled, his fingers alighting on my thighs.

All thoughts faded to carnal desires as I lowered my hips onto his. I dug my fingernails into his shoulders as the first shudders of pleasure overtook me. I set my own pace, refusing to let him guide our rhythm, burying my fingers into his hair.

"Starving?" he breathed.

"Shut up."

The aggressions, frustrations, and inadequacies I'd held on to for so long—I took them out on him with every thrust, every pulse of my body. I held nothing back and he accepted it all eagerly. The sensual moans I drew from him mimicked my own. I kissed, bit, clawed, nipped, and dragged him through all of my cravings. And he watched me...gods, his gaze as he watched me...I was reforged in his flames.

"I'm...almost—" he began and I cut him off.

"Not yet you're not."

I wouldn't let him. I would tease and torture him for as long as I wanted. Any time he attempted to take control I took it back. It was empowering, all-consuming.

When I drew close to climax I told him so, my pace quickening. I let him take my hips and assume his own speed. He orgasmed and it drove me over the edge—my entire body clenching against his. Sounds I didn't recognize escaped my lips and he pressed his mouth to mine. I don't know how long we kissed—the throb of my nerves slowed with my breathing.

"So...dinner?" I asked eventually.

"Alright," he laughed. We redressed and shared a beautiful evening in Valford.

It was the first of many evenings we would spend in each other's arms.

VI

few weeks after our first night spent together, Adrien requested for me to bring a missive to my father. I was uncertain of its contents, but knew the familiar road to Maura and would do anything he asked of me. I hadn't spoken with my parents since I'd left for the university and hoped the trip may remedy the familial ties I'd abandoned.

It was a short visit, but seeing my mother was a joy. I also took the time to visit Lord Radcliff to thank him for all of his teachings and the astrolabe. I spared him the details of my leaving, but I believe he could read it in my tone. My father offered me little conversation—only a return letter for Adrien and a grim smile.

Father hadn't sealed the parchment, and during my return to Valford, I read it.

The wisp has been dealt with. Thank you for looking after Isabelle.

The wisp. The Whisper. Sylus…he'd 'dealt' with Sylus.

I never knew if I should be upset with Adrien or my father. Either way, Sylus was dead. He would never find me.

My position in Adrien's estate mixed between acting as his assistant, his servant, his lover and his confidant. I spent my days running his business and estate, then my evenings sharing his bed.

It was a life I grew accustomed to and wouldn't have traded for anything. I loved him deeply and my affections seemed reciprocated.

At least…for six years.

Upon his arrival home from a trip to Anastas—one he made quite often—his mood was sour. He explained it away as a simple argument with his brother, Jeremi. However, his usual attentions for me were different. He wasn't as affectionate, as kind. His touch was rough and fervent—actions I didn't associate with him. I thought nothing of it and attributed it to a falling out with the brother he cared for, but his attitude continued.

One evening, Adrien pulled me aside after my daily tasks and handed me a sealed scroll.

"I need you to take this to your father. Immediately," he instructed.

"I'll leave at first light then—"

"No, Isabelle I need you to leave now. Ride through the night if you can."

"…Alright." I could never deny him anything. He turned to take his leave and I caught him by the sleeve. "Adrien, what's going on?"

"It's nothing to worry yourself over, little rose." He smiled easily, the Adrien I loved shining through. "If you need to stop, I understand. However, it's an urgent business matter that Garrett needs to be made aware of as soon as possible."

Of course I left that night and of course I rode through until dawn. I wanted to meet Adrien's expectations. When I made it to Maura in three days' time and handed my father the scroll, he read it and offered me a handful of words that I would never forget.

"Isabelle…You should be careful when you're playing with fire."

I stayed at my parent's estate for two weeks on my mother's recommendation. She wanted to fill in the gaps between when I left home to when I found myself living at Adrien's. I was concerned about not being present to maintain his estate, but when she pointed out to me that they existed without me for so long, I conceded.

Father went out of town on business and the time was a much-needed reprieve from my responsibilities as Adrien's assistant. With my father gone, my mother and I shared our time together talking and enjoying Maura in a way I'd never been able to with her. Our conversations made me realize just how long I'd been away—I'd grown up, and we both knew it. I was reintroduced to my mother as an adult, not the cantankerous youth that she knew over a decade before.

When I took my leave, it was much harder than my previous brief trips to Maura. My father hadn't yet returned, but I promised my mother I'd visit soon. Having run myself ragged to make the best time I could to Maura, I took my time going back to Valford. It set me back a day longer than usual, but I had nothing urgent to deliver from my father.

I heard his voice behind one of the guest room doors and entered without a second thought. What awaited me there sparked an anger within me that I didn't realize I still harbored.

"Adrien—" My words froze.

Beside him was a half-naked young woman stepping into the skirts of a servant uniform. A half-naked Whisper. The way he looked at her and his disheveled clothing…they told me everything I needed to know.

"I wasn't aware you were hiring a…new girl." *A Whisper,* I wanted to say.

"Isabelle, you're late," Adrien sighed. "I've told you, when I need you here it's not up for discussion."

"I'm…sorry, m'lord." The nonchalance of his tone stung. This wasn't the welcome I'd expected. I watched his new bedmate struggle with the strings of her corset.

"Don't let it happen again, I mean it."

"Who is she?" I ignored him, fury slowly burning away any relief I had upon reaching the estate.

"My name is Josselyn Thorn. I'm—"

"A Whisper." The word tasted like poison.

The same man who had ordered Sylus killed not only brought another Whisper into the estate but stared at her like some mythical creature.

"Isabelle, you will address Josselyn as if you're speaking to me." It was a warning, a threat.

"Is that so?" *How dare he!*

"Lady Thorn will be living here from now on. You will attend to her every need. Do you understand me?" Another command.

"…Of course, m'lord."

"Go get dressed and find Lily before she burns down the kitchen." He shook his head and dismissed me.

I feared the words that danced on my tongue threatening to spill over. I looked over Josselyn once more and turned to leave.

I wanted to scream. To pull Adrien from the room and demand an explanation. Some tiny part of me wanted so badly to give him the benefit of the doubt. However, his attitude toward me before I left told me he'd planned this. He needed me gone to bring her home.

An inferno of anger consumed me as I returned to my chambers to change out of my travel leathers. I picked up a vase Adrien had purchased for me in Anastas years before and threw it to the floor. The sound of shattering glass was cathartic, but not nearly enough.

Just like every other man in my life, Adrien would use me and forget me. I'd played with fire and found myself once again burned.

EPILOGUE

The building in Anastas that officiated Ring ceremonies was small and out of the way of the city. The outside was underwhelming—no more than a plain stone structure without signage or declaration of what was held there. However, on entry, the decorations and lighting were stunning. Fresh flowers, gold filigree statues, and carvings filled the welcoming entrance. Lush carpets that were heavenly soft on our bare feet lined the floors. I briefly wondered how such a place could maintain itself with the few ceremonies it held each year, but when Cyprus and Josselyn paid for the service, the amount explained away my curiosity.

"Are you ready?" Josselyn asked, taking my hand.

Cyprus' fingers also intertwined with mine and I met each of their gazes.

It was a relationship I'd never imagined for myself—finding love simultaneously reciprocated from both a man and another woman. From two Whispers. We'd been through hell and found solace in each other, our bonds forged in a fire that would never cease to burn.

"Yes...I'm ready," I smiled.

Hands linked, we passed beneath the door to the main hall.

The building was bigger than I'd given it credit for. Before us lay a long run of carpets, divided into three sections via different colored fabrics. Lining each side were multiple tiny, bubbling fountains. The entire room was decked in more fresh flowers and the aroma was incredible. The sounds of the fountains soothed my nerves and the overall ambiance of the room slowed my racing heart. An angelic woman in a stunning white dress stood at the opposite end of the room, her hands clasped and resting against the front of her gown. She offered us a brilliant smile and bowed her head in greeting.

"Cyprus Reyner, Isabelle Rhodes and Josselyn Thorn, welcome to the temple of Rings." She spread her arms, palms open, acknowledging not only us but our surroundings. "Isabelle, shall we begin?"

Despite having each had their own Ring ceremony, Cyprus and Josselyn told me nothing of the proceedings. They wanted me to experience it for myself.

"Yes, please," I replied, squeezing the hands that held mine.

"The three of you have chosen to walk through this life together as one. In all of you exists a love for each other that transcends this plane of existence and weaves you together in one unbreakable bond. In life you'll never part, in death, you'll reunite once more. Once chosen and accepted as a Ring, you declare before myself and the gods that your loyalty will never waver.

Josselyn Thorn—" she turned to Josselyn "—will you protect, love, and care for Isabelle through sickness and in health? Will you share with her and Cyprus both unconditional love and acceptance of their failures and their triumphs?"

"I will. For all of my days." Josselyn smiled at us both, setting my heart alight.

"You may approach," she said. We stepped from the first section of carpet, Cyprus and Josselyn stopping me at the next.

"Cyprus Reyner, will you give your all for these women in both your hardships and joys? Will you promise your heart and mind to them in a way that you share with no other?"

"I will. For all of my days," Cyprus responded, his voice caressing my skin.

"You may approach." We stepped forward again to the third section of carpet.

"Isabelle Rhodes, will you accept your position as their Ring for all time? Will you agree to take no future Husband or Wife? Will you share your fears, your happiness, and your self with Cyprus and Josselyn for as long as you may live?"

"I will. For all of my days," I replied as they had. The elation that emanated from them both was contagious. I couldn't help but smile.

"You may approach." She moved aside as our bare feet shifted to cool, smooth marble.

A short table surrounded by three cushions awaited us. A golden, jeweled goblet filled with dark red wine was placed in its center. Josselyn and Cyprus knelt on the pillows and I followed their lead. The woman sat across from me, lifted the goblet and handed it to Josselyn. Once Josselyn took a drink, she passed it to me. I followed suit before handing it to Cyprus. He also took a drink and placed it back on the table.

"This is the first cup of many the three of you will share throughout your lives. Remember to always be kind, patient, and understanding of one another. Never let anger overrule your love and remember that time is the healer of all things. As overseen by myself and dictated by fate, Isabelle Rhodes has joined this union as a Ring. My lady, may I see your left hand?"

She pulled a small box from beneath the table as Josselyn and Cyprus shifted so their skin touched mine. Cyprus kissed my cheek and Josselyn laid her head on my shoulder. Nothing had ever felt as sure or solid as the love I held for them both. They stayed as close against me as possible and caressed me affectionately while the woman carefully sealed my decision in ink upon my finger.

A few hours later we lay in the soft grass behind our estate, clothing discarded who knows where. Only the stars—*my* stars— were witness to our lovemaking and I wouldn't have it any other way. I lay in between them, Josselyn's head resting on my shoulder, Cyprus arm beneath my neck. I raised my hand above my head, studying the intricate tattoo that newly decorated my finger. Cyprus did the same, leaning his hand against mine, and Josselyn followed suit. The stars sparkled between the spaces of our fingers. Our tattoos designs contained nuanced differences, but to us, they linked us together.

My lovers. My Ring.

RAUCOUS

HILDE'S STORY

To my editors, my biggest fans,
Hilde's story is dedicated to you.

I

Summers were always hard at the Cursed Elixir. Most folks went out of town to enjoy the weather of neighboring cities, giving Anastas a much-needed break. Alan and I though, we always stayed and took the time to polish up the place for the fall and winter months. Thankfully, some of our favorite customers stuck around through the solstice. Without them, our little tavern wouldn't be able to operate during the slow times.

On the evening of the Night of Brynn, Josselyn, Isabelle, and Cyprus joined us. The tavern was empty, as we'd expected—Brynn was typically celebrated in the peace and quiet of people's homes. But these three…well, it seemed they liked to break all the rules. Maybe I shouldn't've told them, but it was part of what made me like them so much.

"Well, well, if it isn't my three favorite troublemakers." I laughed, moving to the door to take their cloaks.

Cyprus flashed me his token smile—like he was always up to something. Josselyn curtsied, ladylike as she was. Finally Isabelle. That young woman was protective of her lovers like a wildcat—I could see it in the way she clung to them and her guarded smile. They made a gorgeous trio, always turning heads in my tavern. On the holiday, however, they found the establishment was empty. It didn't dampen their mood at all.

"What did you do to scare everyone away, Hilde?" Isabelle laughed.

"I'm not sure if you realize, but it *is* a holiday m'lady," I replied.

"I'm sure if Brynn had a choice, she'd be here in the Cursed Elixir with us," Cyprus offered.

"With company like ours? I don't know about that." Josselyn giggled and they took a seat in their favorite booth. I never saw them sit anywhere else.

I made my way toward the cellars for their usual wine when Josselyn hollered an offer. "Hilde! You and Alan should join us for dinner!"

I loved to share conversation with the three of them and it wasn't often we had the chance to talk. Every night for supper was packed—not that we didn't need the business. But it didn't offer much time to chat.

"Alright, dear, let me fetch him," I replied.

I went to the back to grab my husband from his normal kitchen duties. We'd let his help have the night off since we'd expected a slow evening from the years before. My sweet little Alan, stooped over the cooking fire, prodding at the coals to stoke them into living. His dark hair, though tied back, spilled over one shoulder.

"Sweetheart, Josselyn asked us to join them for dinner. What do you say?" I toweled off my hands on my apron.

He murmured a few choice words at the coals that refused to light before wiping the sweat from his brow with one thin arm.

"Will the other customers be alright?" he asked, straightening his back.

"There aren't other customers, love. Just us tonight."

"Alright, then." He nodded, tossing the poker aside and abandoning his attentions to the fire.

I picked up a basket of bread and a plate of meats and cheeses, dropping it off at the table before heading into the cellar for the bottles of wine. When I returned, Isabelle already had Alan laughing. She had a wit sharp as a needle. I opened the first two bottles and poured our glasses full before sitting next to Alan. He kissed my cheek, the frustration of his battle with the fires gone from his face.

"Hilde, how did you come to own this place?" Cyprus gestured at the wide expanse of the hall.

"Yes, you've never told me how you and Alan opened the Cursed Elixir!" Josselyn chimed in, Isabelle nodding her agreement.

"Gods, that feels like an eternity ago," Alan reminisced, his brown eyes focused on something above our table.

"I just can't imagine doing this volume of business on your own," Isabelle remarked. "After working at a place with half as many customers, I don't know how you keep up, Hilde."

I laughed, taking a drink from my own goblet. "When you've been doing this for as long as I have, it gets easier."

"Then tell us!" Josselyn cried, filling her plate with foods from the platter.

"Alright, alright. It started when I was just a girl…"

II

rowing up in Steller's Mill wasn't the easiest thing for a young girl, but my family made the best of it. I had eight brothers and I was the middle child. I was raised never knowing how to be a lady—my siblings made sure of that. We wrestled, slung mud, worked our fingers to the bone and beat each other with anything we could find. I think most of us respected our parents but gods bless it if we weren't a handful.

From the day I was born, my parents ran the only tavern in the town. It was expected that when we were old enough to wash dishes, we'd work there with them for a pittance—our weekly allowance. It was difficult work and not made for children, but it was all they had. My brothers taught me to serve food, haul kegs, and how to treat patrons. I learned to love the life, the people, the atmosphere, and when I came of age, there was nothing else I wanted more than a tavern to call my own. But as it was, competing with my parents' business would be foolish. Since we were on the outskirts of the City of Ends, I decided to try to scout there first.

The days in that city were bright and crowded, the nights loud and bawdy. I wasn't sure how I felt about the citizens as they seemed to turn from kind and open in the daytime to clever and deceitful at night. I allowed a full week's time to really get a feel for the place and that's when I met Alan.

On a sunny afternoon, I stopped by one of the markets near the sea. That's where I saw Alan. Deft hands and deep brown eyes, concentrating on the fish he filleted like an art form. I knew, at that moment…he was the one…

"Really?" Alan interrupted me, nearly sputtering his wine.

"You clearly knew how to use your hands," I replied, refilling his glass.

"That's the moment that you thought, 'I will marry this stringy, sullen man who smells like fish?'" He laughed.

"Not much of a romantic, are you Alan?" Josselyn commented.

"It's not that, I just…it's a little unbelievable," Alan remarked.

"Things aren't always so simple," Cyprus said, cryptic as always.

"So you saw him cutting up fish and then what?" Isabelle interjected.

"Well…"

I approached the counter, shaking like a leaf. I'd been around men all my life but Alan, he was something else.

"Excuse me...can I ask you a few things?" I chanced, eyes constantly wandering his face.

"What's that?" His tone was flat until his eyes met mine. "...M...my lady?"

"Oh, no. Goodness no. That's all wrong," Alan interjected.

"That's exactly how it went! Alan you great coward, hush!" I countered.

"Alright, love, I'm sorry." He tipped his glass to mine.

"How long have you been a fishmonger?" I asked, watching his fine carving work.

"Only a couple years, m'lady. My family needed the coin."

"What did you do before this?"

"I cooked at home. My father and brothers are hunters and I learned to prepare the animals they caught. I...I really enjoy cooking."

"May I ask your name?" It didn't matter that he was a half head shorter than me. I was more scared than when I'd wrestled a bull.

"Alan Olrick, m'lady."

"What do you think of starting a tavern, Alan?" I asked sheepishly.

"Gods, don't start one here. Look at Anastas. I've heard they're growing quickly."

"You seem to know a lot about this place. Would you mind, well…maybe talking with me about your ideas over dinner?"

"I…I would like that very much."

"And that was the night you told me 'anything but fish,'" I said, chuckling.

"You make me sound like a damsel in distress," Alan replied, tearing off a piece of bread from one of the loaves I brought out.

"You were so shy! I had to drag you on our first few outings!" I cried.

"Drag is right. I think you would have carried me in your arms if I let you!"

"Alan!" I rebuked.

"Tell me it's not true!"

Josselyn, Isabelle, and Cyprus politely covered their mouths in their hands. I could tell they were laughing.

I sighed and rolled my eyes. "Fine. But after our first few dates…"

We moved to Anastas in search of a better life. Together. There was an older, recently vacant building that had previously served as a brothel. We scraped every coin between us to purchase it—

"This building was a *brothel*?" Isabelle laughed.

"It was. Spacious, two stories, nice lighting, and good rooms? It fit what we needed," Alan explained methodically.

"Anastas is apparently above that…'*filth*'. So we took it over. And named it as such," I added.

"A place where your ailments are mended, but at what cost?" Cyprus mused. "It's perfect."

"Exactly," I nodded. "And it's served that purpose for years."

Patrons came and went, but those who stayed, those were the ones most important to us. Earning their respect was another story.

III

fter a few months, the real troublemakers showed themselves. Those that couldn't hold their liquor appeared in the tavern. The lightweights who challenged anyone bigger or stronger. Well, I wasn't about to be their usual haunt.

"Jacob, your damn wedding cost me five hundred gold! When are you going to pay up?" One man started hollering one night.

"I'm sorry David. I just…I'm still working on it."

"Then how did you pay for a trip to Maura like it was nothing?"

The argument came to blows. It was an ugly fight that near every patron found themselves a part of, but I stopped it as soon as possible. I pulled David, the smaller of the two, off of Jacob, and kicked them both out of the Cursed Elixir. Of course, with a few choice curses and furious threats, neither of them dared come back to the tavern. I think their bruises and cuts that they bore gave them enough of an idea that I would never allow that behavior.

"You threw out two men…at the same time?" Josselyn asked in disbelief.

"I don't accept that kind of behavior in here," I replied.

"I think what Josselyn means," Isabelle studied the length of my arms before her eyes returned to my face. "...You know, never mind. What next?"

"Well, Alan and I have a great time of running the Elixir, no matter the crowd that comes in. We'll always accept those willing to give up their hard-earned coin."

"Not as romantic as you thought, is it?" Alan commented.

"Maybe that's not fair," I reassessed. "We'll always accept patrons who give a damn about one another."

"So you're living your dream, then?" Cyprus smiled.

"Absolutely, wouldn't trade it for the world." I toasted the table.

We shared an incredible evening the likes of which I'd not had in ages. That Night of Brynn, I thanked the goddess for our companionship, for my tavern...

For Alan.

Catherine LaCroix is the author of multiple award-winning fantasy stories, including *The Whispers of Rings, Little Treasures,* and *The Silent Note.* She resides in Glendale, Arizona with her four rabbits and a seemingly never-ending stock of wine. Connect with her through **www.whispersfromcat.com** or e-mail her at **whispersfromcat@gmail.com**

SPECIAL THANKS TO:

Marlena Mozgawa: My fantastic cover artist. You can contact
Marlena at lenamo.art@gmail.com

Natsuki, Pete, Chris, Mom and Dad, Luke, Ryan, and Ryne
The Kingdom of Rhoryn would be such a lonely place without all
of you

My Readers
Seeing these characters through your eyes bring them to life for me.
Thank you so much for your continued support.